C000226390

The Bishop of San Fernando

For Kit, John,
Jenny and Norman

The Bishop of
San Fernando

a novel by

David McLaurin

Duckworth

First published in 1994 by
Gerald Duckworth & Co. Ltd.
The Old Piano Factory
48 Hoxton Square, London N1 6PB
Tel: 071 729 5986
Fax: 071 729 0015

© 1994 by David McLaurin

All rights reserved. No part of this publication
may be reproduced, stored in a retrieval system, or
transmitted, in any form or by any means, electronic,
· mechanical, photocopying, recording or otherwise,
without the prior permission of the publisher.

A catalogue record for this book is available
from the British Library

ISBN 0 7156 2625 6

Typeset by Ray Davies
Printed in Great Britain by
Redwood Books , Trowbridge

1

THE BISHOP of San Fernando intended to pass the twentieth anniversary of his episcopal appointment alone. He had arrived in San Fernando alone that day twenty years before, and ever since, the anniversary – the 8th December, the feast of the Immaculate Conception – had acquired a solitariness about it. It was known that he did not celebrate Mass in the Cathedral in public on that day. How that became known, he did not know. Solitude, that most unapostolic of dispositions, had a way of establishing itself. You found yourself to be alone; people presumed you wished to be alone and dared not interrupt you; and all of a sudden you were enclosed in a carapace of isolation, which was not of your own making. He had once been a social man, too social, perhaps. His parents had been the sort of people who gave the impression that they were forever at parties, or preparing to go to parties, or recovering from them. As a very young child, he had no clear memory of his mother at all, but he would have liked to have been able to remember her coming to kiss him goodnight after his nurse had put him to bed; and he would dwell on the warmth of her kiss, the gleam of her pearls in the twilight and an impression of coloured silk, as if he could really remember them.

His father he connected – in fact, not fiction – with uniforms, for he had been a magistrate and the Chief of the Port of Spain police, and dinner jackets that smelled of stale cigars. He had been acclaimed as the handsomest man in Trinidad: he had been told that by old ladies after the Second World War. And his mother had been beautiful. They had taken it as a personal slight when he had told them he wanted to be a priest. He had had the impression that they thought he had failed them.

In this place – San Fernando – they called him English. His name was English. He had been christened Alfred (after his grandfather) George (after the King) Edward (after a recently deceased beloved dog of his parents). His surname, not given but inherited, was Palmer-Ross. It had enough weight to it to make it what the Bishop supposed other people would call 'a good name', the sort associated with the fringes of the aristocracy. Some assumed that he was an English gentleman. Yet he was not English at all – his mother had been a South American of Welsh extraction. On his father's side, his grandmother had been a Scottish doctor's daughter from British Guiana. His grandfather had been more Dutch and French than English. This mixture made him nothing less than Trinidadian.

He had inherited much of his parents' looks. As a young man he had shared much of their disposition. He had been noticed; and at the very early age of thirty-six he had been made a bishop. He owed this honour to two things: a general sense among the clergy of the island that he deserved recognition for his talents – for he had a way of pleasing that never aroused jealousy in the less fortunate; and, more important, without trying to he had won the favour of the Papal Nuncio of the day. It was the Papal Nuncio's job to forward names to Rome; his name had been forwarded; three months later he had been ordained by the Pope himself, in Rome. He had spent an enjoyable year in Rome as a Vatican diplomat – and then he had been appointed Bishop of San Fernando, a post he had kept for twenty years – for at the age of thirty-seven, without his knowing it, his career had stopped. He had been a shooting star – a brief spurt of glory, followed by interminable oblivion.

That he was a failure – for he was not a good bishop, even of San Fernando – that he was a failure was a thought that always struck him forcefully on the anniversary of his arrival. But today, his solitude was to be interrupted. He had received disquieting news. The day before an unfamiliar voice had spoken to him over the telephone. The voice had called him 'Alfred' with the peculiar emphasis on the final syllable that marked all Trinidadian

6

speech. With some surprise he realised that his interlocutor was the Archbishop of Port of Spain and was inviting himself to lunch for the 8th. The Archbishop explained that he was passing through San Fernando and would stop off on his way. Only when he had put the telephone down, did he realise the fraudulence of this arrangement. No one passed through San Fernando. It was the end of the line for there was no other place beyond it. It lay on the route to nowhere. It invited no one to stop off. The Archbishop's careless lie had been intended to cover up some sort of embarrassment. And then all was clear. The Archbishop was coming to San Fernando to sack him. After twenty years of limbo – the best years of his life – his life was to start again.

Of course, bishops were not sacked, at least not any more. Pope Paul VI of happy memory had laid down that they were to retire at the age of seventy-five – which would give Alfred another nineteen years of episcopal service. Nineteen years remained to him and would have to be filled in somehow. Perhaps they would invent some post for him: the Pontifical Commission for Tourism was full of misfits such as himself. If he was lucky he might get sent back to Rome; or else he might end up somewhere less familiar – Dublin, Louvain or Montreal – where he would grow old and die, and where no one would know of his shame.

The Bishop's shame was a young man of twenty-seven called Simon Palmer. He bore but half his name. He was a secret known to very few people, rather like the identity of the Man in the Iron Mask. The Archbishop was the only living person who now knew; he had heard it from the Papal Nuncio who had passed it on as a matter of duty. The Papal Nuncio was long since dead. In all the Nuncio's diplomatic career Simon Palmer was the only thing that had rankled. He had never seen him, and wished that he had never heard of him. For the discovery of his existence had blighted the episcopal career of the man he had chosen before it had really begun.

What had happened was this. Before being ordained by the Pope, Alfred Palmer-Ross had made a retreat of seven days, as was the custom. At the end of the seven days doubt had crept

7

into his mind about his suitability as a bishop. The ordination was still a month distant. True, it had been announced in the *Osservatore Romano*, but it could still be cancelled. Alfred, true to his training, resolved to submit himself to the judgment of another. From the convent in Frascati where he was staying, he wrote to the Papal Nuncio in Trinidad. His choice was simple: the Nuncio had decided to make him a bishop – let him decide whether a seven-year-old boy was a barrier or not. The letter had been sent, but no reply had come. He had gone ahead with the ordination, not knowing that the day the Pope's hands made him a bishop was the very day the Nuncio got his letter, thanks to the inefficiency of the Italian post. And thus he had been made a bishop and become an embarrassment to the Church all at once. The Nuncio naturally had no choice but to bury him in San Fernando as soon as was discreetly possible. Although Alfred had never believed it possible, others would always fear scandal. And besides, the fact that he was a priest with a child meant that he was innately unworthy of a position of trust. And so he had been buried alive. Now it seemed the Archbishop was on his way to find him a more suitable burial spot.

*

The Archbishop arrived at noon precisely. He was a short man, swarthy of skin, and he walked up the wooden steps to the house with short precise movements. Once inside the hallway, he wiped his brow with a white handkerchief which still left him looking like the oily Levantine he really was. Yet, reflected Alfred, as he politely stooped to kiss the air an inch above his hand, he was a kind man really – there were worse archbishops.

'Alfred,' said the Archbishop.

'Your Grace,' he replied. He did wish the Archbishop would not use his Christian name. It was so very post-Vatican II. Pope Paul VI had called him 'Monsignor' when they had made the *ad limina* visit to Rome, but the Archbishop would never be so formal, he feared. Once one-sided familiarity was established there was no going back.

'Lunch,' said Alfred, 'is at 12.15.'

He led his guest into the sitting-room, a spacious room of polished wood which contained six hard throne-like chairs gathered round an old-fashioned radiogram.

'I should have made some rum punch,' said Alfred once they had settled into this joyless ambience.

'Oh no,' said the Archbishop – a little too quickly. 'I mean, not unless you wanted to.'

'I – that is, such a thought never occurred to me.'

'This room seems little used,' said the Archbishop.

'That is so,' conceded Alfred. 'It was last used when Your Grace was here ten years ago.'

'Of course, you know, each bishop has more or less *carte blanche* in his own diocese,' began the Archbishop a little defensively. 'I would never dream of interfering with San Fernando. People talk about you from time to time in Port of Spain, and I have never once said to myself, "Alphonsus – you must go to San Fernando and see what Bishop Palmer-Ross is up to." Never once. I just listened, was curious and wondered.'

'And what were they saying?' asked Alfred uneasily.

'Nothing remotely scandalous. Distance, in your case, breeds respect. No one has seen you for twenty years in Port of Spain. They say that you've become a sort of saint.'

'Oh really.'

'No. Indeed. Let me tell you what they say about you. They say that you were the most intelligent and well-educated bishop in the West Indies and yet you gave it all up to work in the slums of San Fernando.'

'I don't work in slums. I don't work. The Vicar-General does most of the work. I haven't given anything up. I just happen to be a bishop who's unemployable. I imagine you've come here to prevail upon me to resign.'

'Not at all.'

A bell tinkled.

'Lunch,' said Alfred abruptly.

They went back into the hallway and into another equally bare room. Two places were laid at the table. The food had been left out for them. In the background a door shut. Alfred said grace.

'You shouldn't be cross when people think you are a saint,' began Alphonsus again. 'They may be right. Of course, you don't think you are a saint because you don't feel you are a saint. Here you are, twenty years of solitude and prayer, and all you have to show for it is a deep sense of emptiness. I know. You see, I'm the opposite, always cheerful, and I know very well that our virtue and our dispositions have nothing to do with each other. You could very well be a saint, even if you reproach yourself unendingly; in fact I'd say that a deep feeling of unworthiness is often a sign of sanctity.'

'I don't reproach myself,' said Alfred. 'At least not in the sense you mean. I think I've been a fool and am a fool, but I hardly ever think of sin. It's unchristian to reproach oneself for past sins that have been forgiven. God forgives and that is that. To keep on going over the past is to doubt God's ability to forgive.'

'Good. That is excellent. Then why do you live like this? The Vicar-General tells me you live like a monk. It's terrible. You never go out: no parish visitations – and San Fernando is a small diocese.'

'My poor Vicar-General,' said Alfred. 'I think he's given up on me. He's supposed to help me, and he finds I don't want any help. He is supposed to be second in command and he finds the chief's place is empty. Yes, I've abdicated my responsibilities. You are right to be annoyed with me.'

'I am not annoyed with you.'

'You ought to be. I ought to be doing all the things bishops are supposed to do, and yet I do next to nothing. I am a bishop and no one rebukes me for my idleness. They have too much respect. Even you, dear Archbishop, are a little frightened of me. Otherwise you would have got me out of here years ago. Or perhaps I'm wrong – perhaps you have tried and nothing came of it – the Nuncio said you had to put up with me.'

10

'He did,' said the Archbishop with candour. 'He said you were to stay here for as long as you filled the post without any other difficulties.'

'I see. And as I am forced to be bishop here, I might as well be a saint bishop. Perhaps that is why you are here – to test my sanctity. Or perhaps you have come here because you think I've gone mad. It is a form of madness, shutting yourself away for twenty years.'

'But you are not so entirely shut away, are you? And, as I've said, I've come here for a concrete reason. I told you that. I haven't come here to pry. This curry is quite good, you know. May I help myself to some more?'

'A concrete reason?'

'Your Vicar-General – '

'Has made some sort of complaint?'

'Yes,' said the Archbishop. 'But not about you! He complains of old age. He is seventy-five after all; he has decided to retire. I have accepted his resignation – I mean, I think he ought to retire. And it is about his replacement that I have come to talk to you today.'

'You have chosen someone?'

'Not yet. But there is a young priest who strikes me as suitable.'

'Naturally I'd be only too happy to have whoever you wished. It's the least I could do. San Fernando has an unapostolic bishop, so it deserves the best Vicar-General it can have.'

'It does. And so do you.'

'Then all is settled,' said Alfred. 'What is the young man called?'

'Father John Salvatori. I think – '

'Forgive me, Your Grace. How did you know that I have not been entirely alone? I presume you mean to say that – that a certain young man has been here.'

'Simon Palmer? We can use his name, I think,' said the Arch-bishop. 'He wrote and told me, of course. I confirmed him, you know, fifteen years ago. He's a nice boy. And when he told me that he was coming to San Fernando I told him to go and see the

11

Bishop. He wrote and told me about the visit just to say that he'd carried it out.'

Alfred got up from the table. The windows were shuttered against the heat and there was no distant scene to comfort him. He was forced to try and glimpse the outside between wooden slats. There was silence in the room for some time.

'I suppose I should be grateful for all you have done,' he said at last. 'The young man spoke about you so very highly. You confirmed him; he told me that. You confirmed him when he was at the College in Port of Spain. You were kind to him because he was a poor fatherless boy. You make me feel ashamed.'

'Why?'

'Because my own conduct is so very odd. So unfatherly. He told me that his mother had died. I had no idea. It was very strange hearing about her after twenty-seven years of silence. She had died three years previously for him – but many years previously for me. And the young man – Simon Palmer. I had shut out all thoughts of his existence. I didn't want him to exist. His existence ruined everything for me. If he'd never been born I would not be here now. Why did you send him to see me?'

'I thought it would do you good to see him – to see that he hadn't turned out badly.'

'With such parentage – could anyone turn out well?' asked Alfred.

*

Simon Palmer had known about illegitimacy from quite an early age. It was something you learned at school. At the College in Port of Spain, where English history was taught to Trinidadian boys by Catholic priests, he had learned about Elizabeth Tudor. She had been illegitimate, a usurper. And yet she had been remarkably successful. The very legitimate Mary Stuart had always commanded Catholic support: but Simon's support for her had waned when – at about twelve years of age – he had discovered that he too was a bastard, and he had thrown his lot in with Good Queen Bess.

Realisation had come slowly. The absence of a father had never been keenly felt, for what he had not known he could not miss. There were no dim childhood memories of a male presence in the house. Home had meant his mother, and she had never even mentioned the word 'father' to him. It was as if he had been the result of a virginal conception. That was impossible, as the Virginal Conception could never be repeated. Miracles were not made to order. Nevertheless, Simon knew that there was something special in his birth. He was different from his mother. His hair was rather dark, very fine and very straight. His nose and lips, the entire shape of his head was somehow different. He was a sort of dark European. She was a pale sort of black. For the first ten years of his life he had assumed that this meant that he was not his mother's race at all; that he was some sort of throwback, a freak who resembled a white ancestor generations back, except that he was not entirely white. Sometimes he speculated on the possibility that he was a completely different race from his mother altogether, and that he was a changeling. Only when he was told the secrets of sex did he realise that he was the result of a racial mixing and that his father must have been white.

As he progressed through the College, the odd idea of this non-existent father would strike him from time to time. He supposed him to be English. When he read *Henry V* he imagined this unknown parent as a gentleman in bed in England on Crispin's Day. Or he thought of him wandering lonely as a cloud, in the middle distance, faceless. Anything English would remind him with a jolt that he too was half-English. Except that it wasn't true. He was Trinidadian. England was a land he would never see.

It had never occurred to him to ask his mother about this mysterious putative Englishman. There was something in her dreamy eyes that discouraged enquiry. She herself was a woman who never questioned nor expected to be questioned. She had been born and bred in Tobago. In Port of Spain she kept a fent-shop. He wondered whether his mother had chosen the type of shop she wanted to keep. It sold highly respectable cloth – by the yard. It was hard to associate his mother with any sexual

13

lapse, when you saw her demurely measuring out the calico day after day. Her life had been one of measuredness, he now thought. She had died leaving no clue to the mystery of his own coming to be.

Trinidad was full of illegitimate people. Hundreds were conceived every Carnival. Yet, in his mother's respectable routine he detected a desire to hide his illegitimacy. It was never spoken of. And truly, he supposed, in wedlock was better than out of it.

This realisation of bastardy, this mark of difference, had come at about the same time as his confirmation. It had always been the custom for the Archbishop to visit the College before the ceremony and interview candidates at random. Alphonsus Nourganian, Archbishop of Port of Spain, a short ill-favoured man, yet every inch an Archbishop, Levantine yet dignified, had questioned boys about the seven gifts of the Holy Spirit. Then he had come to Simon and stopped. There was a priest next to him with a list, pointing at the relevant names to give the impression that the Archbishop knew all his flock by name.

'Well,' said the diminutive prelate. 'Do you know which apostle you are named after?'

This question had seemed like a special favour from God. For why should he be singled out? He was no different from any other boy, to look at, at least. It was one of the advantages of being Trinidadian that there was no prototype to fit. He felt an immediate warmth for this rather strange little man, with his pectoral cross and his big ring. There were red buttons on his soutane too. So fascinated were the child's eyes by these details of costume that for some minutes (or rather seconds – yet the whole incident seemed to last much longer, as subsequent callings to mind were to endow it with increasing significance) he wondered what to reply.

He answered the question and His Grace moved on to another boy.

That – if the boy had only known it – was to be the formative moment of his entire youth. As he discovered later, by reading the Bible and the newspapers and the novels of Dickens, there were decisive moments in every life and his encounter with the Archbishop was his. For other people the moment of decision seemed to him to be clear-cut, involving some sort of choice. Abraham could have stayed at home; the man you read about in the papers who chopped his wife up with an axe could have married someone else. But for Simon there was never an either/or dilemma. He had met the Archbishop, and years later he was able to pinpoint that meeting as the ultimate source of the knowledge he had about himself.

He wondered as a young man whether his had been a religious experience. Religious language was one way – the closest perhaps – of expressing his mode of existence. For what he knew about himself was this: he was a stranger and pilgrim on the face of the earth. He was an exile from his true home. That was the religious way of putting it. It expressed it rather well, he always thought. One knew what one meant, but always there was a certain elusiveness, an eternal why.

Why did he think of himself as the frog in the fairy tale, waiting to be transformed by a kiss into a handsome prince? Why did he feel that he was not yet the person he really ought to be, but some sort of being in embryo? And why had he seen the Archbishop as the man who would reveal all to him?

Their friendship had endured for many years, and when Simon was to move to San Fernando it was the Archbishop who told him to go to see Bishop Palmer-Ross. It did not occur to him to consider not going. On a bright November day he had gone to the Bishop's house, rung the bell and, when the surprised black servant opened the door, had presented his letter of introduction. The servant bore it away, having shot him a look of infinite suspicion and saying not a word. He was left in the wooden polished hall, unaware that his visit was momentous, that he had pierced a solitude considered by the housekeeper (and the Archbishop too) as impenetrable. But he was not aware of this. He was only aware of the smell of beeswax and a vague surprise at the bareness of the house. Where the Archbishop lived was far more homely.

15

After some ten minutes the elderly housekeeper returned with a look of the utmost perturbation. The Bishop would see him, she said. She opened a door to the side of the hall and showed him into a room with chairs. It was as cheerless as a dentist's waiting-room. Then she left him. Another five minutes passed. A feeling of unease settled on Simon. Perhaps he had called at an awkward time. Perhaps Bishop Palmer-Ross was busy. And yet the house was completely silent, not at all like the house of a busy man. He could not even hear the ticking of the clock. His sense of unease was confirmed by the hardness of the wooden chair he was sitting in and the discomfort of wearing a collar and tie. But he had thought it better to call on this important stranger formally dressed.

His reflections were interrupted by the entrance of the Bishop. He was a tall thin man with white hair and a pale complexion. He wore a black clerical shirt and a pectoral cross. Despite the relative casualness of his dress, he seemed ill at ease.

'I am sorry to have kept you waiting,' he said, extending a hand.

He seemed startled when Simon bent over his hand to kiss his ring.

'Please do sit down,' he said, when the operation was over.

Simon took his seat again, and the Bishop sat opposite him. He saw the old man (so he seemed to him) stare at him anxiously as if wondering what his face and figure were like, or looking for some resemblance to a recognisable prototype. Simon knew at once that the white bishop – it sounded like a chess piece – wanted to know what side, white or black, he belonged to.

'You are a friend of our Archbishop?' said Alfred.

'Yes, my lord. His Grace is my godfather, only he says he is, "in a manner of speaking". It was he who confirmed me.'

'But he wasn't present at your baptism?'

'No.'

'Then he is just a spiritual godfather, I suppose. That is a useful thing to have, isn't it? Are you going to live here in San Fernando?'

'Yes, my lord. I've been promoted. I work for Da Silva's and they've made me head wages clerk in San Fernando.'

'Then you do clerical work,' said Alfred. 'So do I.'

'It was the Archbishop who recommended that I work for Da Silva's when I was eighteen.'

'You set great store by the Archbishop's advice, I see,' said Alfred. 'That is a good thing.'

'There was no one else to advise me,' he said. 'My mother couldn't, so I listened to the Archbishop.'

'And weren't you sad to leave Port of Spain?'

'The Archbishop advised me to take promotion when I had the chance, my lord.'

'And what did your mother say to your going away?'

'Nothing, she is dead,' he said simply.

'Oh, I am sorry,' said Alfred lightly. This was the first intimation he had that the woman he had once believed he loved was dead. He stood up.

'Come and see me again soon,' he said.

When the door closed on the young man, Bishop Palmer-Ross turned his face to the interior of the house, away from his son, and groaned.

*

It was the memory of this meeting that prompted his question to the Archbishop: 'Could anyone with such parentage turn out well?'

The Archbishop had given no answer; he had not expected one. The Archbishop had merely smiled maddeningly and then departed, telling him to expect the new Vicar-General before Christmas. And Bishop Palmer-Ross was left in his empty house reflecting that the quietness of the last twenty years was irreparably broken.

17

2

MRS PALMER-ROSS, the Bishop's mother, many years before had described San Fernando as the worst place she had ever visited. No one quite knew when or why she had been there – only that she had never gone back. Alfred would call her judgment to mind when he sat on his verandah late at night before going to bed. His mother had been a snob, and cultivated these little fits of disdain. For those who had always lived there, San Fernando was rather like Paris for a Parisian or London for a Londoner – home. One such was the Vicar-General, San Fernando-born, now seventy-five and now sitting on the verandah, admiring a hibiscus illuminated by the gas-lit circle of light in which they sat and beyond which lay the rest of the garden.

'There is no twilight here,' said Alfred.

'What is that?' asked the priest.

'It's the time of day when it's not quite light or quite dark. In England it can last for several hours. But here darkness falls suddenly.'

'Yes. I used to want to see England,' said the old priest.

'Did you? Why?'

'We learned about it at school,' he said. 'Simon de Montfort, Oliver Cromwell and all those no-good Roundheads. I'd like to have gone and seen where they cut off all their heads on Tower Green, but I suppose I never shall. It's a bit ridiculous, isn't it, my lord, to think that sixty years ago all we children were learning about a country that we would never see. I suppose if you haven't your own history then you have to learn someone else's. And that song, "Dis is de chatter, the chatter of the Land". For years I wondered about this chatter and only later did I discover that

18

they meant the Magna Chatter. I'd thought it was like a town-crier before that.'

The Vicar-General grinned. The Bishop poured out some more rum punch. Life was not so bad after all. He had been given the recipe for rum punch many years before, by his godfather. He had not made it for twenty years, but it was one thing that you did not forget. Sitting on the verandah and looking down on the harbour below them – darkness covering the ugliness only too visible by day – one could almost think San Fernando pleasant. Perhaps he should have invited the Vicar-General to drinks before this.

But the old priest was knocking back the last of his punch and getting ready to go. It was as though he was recollecting the fact that he had overstayed his welcome. He had been there an hour. Surely that was enough, or rather the limit of politeness, where a first visit was concerned. And so he left, having made his first and last visit to his Bishop's house. Within a few days he would be gone completely.

Perhaps I frighten people, thought Alfred. Or perhaps they frighten me. It was hard to tell. When one has deliberately decided to live without people for twenty years as he had done, and when after so long an absence they came back, one really had no idea what to make of them.

People came back. One could never quite cut oneself free. With one's family one might. The Palmer-Rosses were quite out of the picture as far as Alfred was concerned. The older generation were all dead. His brothers and sisters were all in England, the United States or Canada. They rather resented the fact that he had become a priest; and they resented that he had not renounced his share of their parents' estate. He had kept control of what was his. Part of that money had gone to the boy's mother. She had bought a fent-shop with it. She had never asked for more.

But though his family was all gone, there were other ties. There was the Church. One would never cease to be a Bishop. One could never undo the past. And one could never undo the

19

fact that he was the boy's father. Only two people on earth knew that – himself and the Archbishop. But even if only he himself had the knowledge, that was enough. He had seen Simon Palmer, and his isolation was breached. The young man could not be ignored, for there was something in him that was his father's, although he had only seen Alfred for the first time when he was twenty-seven years old.

That elusive something that he had inherited had puzzled the Bishop in the intervening weeks. Simon Palmer was a different race from Alfred. That was clear enough, though the young man's appearance, Alfred noted, was certainly not against him: he was a dark European, not a pale African. He was, though, barely educated – he was a clerk in a trading company. He was someone pleased to be a clerk, as far as the Bishop could see. He had spoken with the vowels of Port of Spain – as the Bishop did too to an extent, had he known it. The young man had sat there awkwardly in his clothes, ill at ease. None of these were qualities associated with the Palmer-Ross family. Truly, said Alfred to himself, I am a snob.

Rather, he was half a snob. Snobbery had not saved him from making love twenty-eight years before to a woman of the lower classes. She had been his mother's housekeeper in their house in Tobago. She had had the most beautiful eyes he had ever seen. They had been there together once – after the death of his parents, when he had gone there to oversee the sale of the house. They had been together alone, and he fell.

He did not reproach himself as he sat on his verandah twenty-eight years later. Rather he tried to analyse the reasons for this fall. He had never fallen before. Curiosity had gnawed away at him for the greater part of thirty years. His elder brothers, all three of them, had left examples to make him wonder and be jealous. And when the woman Maria had looked at him in that way he had known that what he always wondered about was in his grasp.

'I love you,' he had told her. He had said the words because they were expected of him in such circumstances. But that had been later. In the first part of the relationship, a first part that had started with holding hands, love in the profane sense had not entered his mind. He had thought that he had providentially stumbled upon something utterly different, a blessed companionship of the type that Adam and Eve had enjoyed before the apple, the snake and the shame of being naked together. The sexual impulse when he felt it, he thought (or convinced himself to think), was something else. And thus he was undone completely, for by the time the sexual impulse arrived in all its undeniable fullness it was too late, for he had not the strength to stop it.

'I love you,' he had said. But he had not meant it. The words had been forced out of him by his conscience and were spoken with difficulty. They covered up the truth of the matter, which was that he desired her. But he clung to the word 'love' even when he knew it was not true. It had to be true. For love covered a multitude of sins. A lover could be forgiven, for to sin out of love was almost excusable. Thus he hid his shame in the second part of their relationship.

At first he tried to reason with himself about the seriousness of his guilt. He loved her. But even if that was not true, he had not planned to sleep with her. There had been no deliberation. It was only a venial sin, an aberration. He would continue to say Mass.

He had returned to Port of Spain, yet promising her that he would come back. He had come back within a few days, convincing himself and the then Archbishop for whom he worked that family business required his presence in Tobago. They had made love again, almost immediately, as soon as he was safely in the house. He had prayed to God for strength against temptation, but it had not come.

It was then that the extent of his fall had dawned upon him. As she clung to him he knew that he was there because he wanted to be there, because he had chosen it. He was as all men were; it was simply not true that he was a man apart. What he was doing now was what they all did – all the men of his type. He was one of them after all.

21

It was a month or two later, in Port of Spain, when he had more or less succeeded in driving his fall from his mind, that he had got her letter. Maria announced that she was having a child. There was a certain dignity in the letter. She did not remind him that he had declared undying love to her, but merely that a certain event – a birth – would take place. He sent her a large cheque and heard no more, except that the cheque was received and the son born, and called Simon Palmer. She had thought he would want to know that the boy was getting one half of his father's surname. She had taken his silence for approval.

*

The rum punch was all gone. It was later, past nine o'clock. The Bishop was usually in bed by then. But he felt a certain diffidence about going to bed when there was so much business outstanding. Down there in the town (the Bishop's house stood on Naparima Hill), where the lights sparkled on the hot December night, was Simon Palmer, who could not be ignored. And soon the new Vicar-General would be here. Alfred now suspected that the new Vicar-General – a man he had never met – a young man – might be rather tiresome. Apart from his name, John Salvatori, he knew nothing about him. The Archbishop had had some ulterior motive perhaps in appointing this young man. Perhaps Alfred had not shown enough interest in the whole matter. Perhaps his indifference had been taken advantage of. Whatever the case, it would be a good idea to see the young man before Salvatori arrived.

He sat down to write a note to Simon Palmer, to invite him to lunch. He reflected that he did not know his address. However, he knew the company he worked for. He stressed the informal nature of the lunch, in the hope that he wouldn't shackle the boy with collar and tie. Then he sealed the letter and resolved to take it down to Da Silva's himself the next morning.

3

EVEN TWENTY YEARS' residence in San Fernando had never really reconciled Alfred to living there. Naparima Hill was made tolerable by the fact that it enjoyed something of a sea breeze, but the town below was dank, fetid and hot. Even the harbour waters seemed to sweat oil; the stagnant sea, unstirred by current and wind, offended the nostrils. The various ships at anchor hardly ever seemed to change, but merely grew heavier with the passing years as barnacles stuck to their keels. There was no swimming because there was no beach, and even beyond the harbour the sea was hardly inviting: it had that churned-up quality that reminded you of coffee, and to touch it felt like milk. This was the fault of the Orinoco, the mud of which polluted the waters for miles around. Tobago had clear waters, and even Port of Spain was a more enviable place.

San Fernando was built on familiar lines. The best houses were at the top of Naparima Hill, and the very worst ones were at the water's edge. The middling ones lay in the middle, crouched around the Cathedral, a ramshackle, not quite Gothic, structure. In typical ecclesiastical fashion the Bishop's house was above the Cathedral and the Vicar-General's house lay next to it.

Alfred Palmer-Ross left home at 7.30 in the morning to call on Simon Palmer, before the rising sun made the town intolerable. He had been up since five that morning; he was always up at five. He had said Mass in his private Chapel, a bare little room containing an altar, almost as bare as the dining-room next door to it. Before Mass he had fulfilled his spiritual duties: he had spent an hour in silent prayer and recited the Breviary as the Church required of him. Now he left the house, dressed in clerical black, with his brass pectoral cross shining on his shirt.

Once in Rome, as a seminarian, he had seen a Bishop wearing his pectoral cross under his shirt. He discovered that this Bishop, a youngish man, had retired from his ministry for reasons of health. This memory always made him wear his cross openly.

Half way down the hill he stopped and entered the Cathedral, something he did but rarely. There was an air of doleful neglect about the place, and a smell of candle-grease mixed with something he could never identify, but which, combined, produced what could only be called the atmosphere and stench of decay. The place was rotting before his eyes. He sat down on the back bench, once again moved by the sheer ugliness of the building. The benches were of a cheap grey wood, the floor was dull and unpolished. The paint was peeling off the walls. Even the statue of Our Lady of Lourdes had a melancholy aspect, despite the candles burning on the stand in front of it. Alfred felt a twinge of embarrassment and wondered what Father Salvatori would say about it when he arrived. Twenty years of episcopal inactivity were clearly reflected in the state of the building. Of course, the upkeep of the Cathedral was not the Bishop's job but the responsibility of the Vicar-General. However, the Vicar-General had had other things to do, as everything in the diocese had devolved upon him. But whoever's fault it was, the dilapidation – if you could use such a word of a wooden church – was an eloquent symbol of his own personal failure. He had failed to be a good Bishop – in fact to be any sort of a Bishop at all. But he was not sure why he had failed. The reason lay in the past; it was connected with the existence of Simon Palmer, but beyond that he could not go. The past was past and could not be changed or redeemed. Thus no matter how much he wanted to act as a Bishop should, or even to be a good Bishop, something impeded him: he could not act, for he was paralysed.

He was sitting by the confession box and wished he could go to confession. He imagined himself saying: 'Bless me, Father, for I have sinned. For twenty years I have not fulfilled the duties of my state ...' But how could he say that? It was true. He had not done his duty. But had he sinned? He did not think he had. Sin implied an intention to do wrong, but he had never intended to be like this, he just was – he had never made a choice. Like a man whose leg had been amputated – it was not his fault. He could not confess his inadequacy because it was the sort of thing that was beyond forgiveness. He was, oddly, the only man in his diocese who was beyond the reach of Divine Grace. Perhaps Divine Grace could help him to accept his condition; they said that people with the most horrible diseases went to Lourdes and came back not cured, but at least at peace. He knew he was not at peace now. But even here there was a contradiction, for how could he be resigned or at peace with something that was so obviously wrong? Being a bad Bishop was not like having cancer; you couldn't offer it up to the Almighty. God did not want it.

It was no use asking the advice of some wise priest, because he knew what the advice would be: he would be told to ignore his disability – if that was the word for it – and to carry on as if it did not exist. This too was impossible. He simply found himself unable to perform confirmations, make pastoral visits and do all the other things people expected of him. All he could bring himself to do was the barest of minimums – to celebrate Mass in the Cathedral twice a year, at Christmas and Easter. The rest of the time he hid.

*

He got up, genuflected and left. The offices of Da Silva were a few minutes' walk away. They were housed in one of the wooden buildings that rendered the town anonymous, so similar were all the houses. Yet Da Silva was the most important business in the town, to judge by the centrality of its offices. Their interior resembled what he had always imagined a Victorian counting-house to look like. It was dark, and after the glare of the waterfront, his eyes had to adjust themselves to the shuttered gloom. Eventually he was able to make out rows of high desks and stools, a slow rotating fan above, and reams of ageing paper which lent the room its predominating sepia colour. It was strange and yet somehow familiar from his childhood reading of Dickens. He did not see Simon, only five or six bored faces poring over what he took to be ledgers. He wondered what they were doing or meant to be doing, for the air hung heavy with idleness in the large room, and even the fan hardly stirred the papers that littered the desks.

'Sir,' said a young man eventually, calling him out of his abstraction.

It was half question and half command. Not quite sure what he was meant to do, he followed the young man, who led him into a small room off the main office. There he was left alone with a red-faced white man who seemed to be of his own age, who sat at a desk with his back to the sunlit window. On the ceiling of this office too a fan rotated, idly chopping at the reflections of the harbour water from outside.

'It is a very great pleasure,' the red-faced man was saying. 'The name is Barratt, Anthony Barratt, always known as Tony.'

'Mr Barratt, I –' began Alfred, wanting to say that he had only come to deliver a letter for the Head Clerk or whatever Simon Palmer was. But a frank admission of this errand seemed rather foolish. Bishops were not supposed to do the work of messenger boys, as Mr Barratt must surely know.

'I expect you recognise the name,' Mr Barratt was saying. 'The fact is that my sister was something of a flame of your brother Hugo. It was a terrible pity about his death; he was a fine fellow and very popular with the ladies. Perhaps you remember her? Pat Barratt? As a matter of fact she married an Englishman and now lives in Bristol. It did cross my mind to call on you when I got here. But of course, one is always so busy. But good of you to come and seek me out first. It is much appreciated.'

'Have you only just arrived then, Mr Barratt?'

'Lord no, I got here twelve years ago. I was thirty then. The whole shebang was in great shape then. Then of course my wife decided to leave me; she said she couldn't stand living here a moment longer. She was a Seacole – perhaps you remember them – they used to live in Maraval. She said she couldn't bear living in a place where nothing ever happened. I agreed with her and said why didn't we both leave it. Of course that wasn't at all what she had in mind. The fact was that she had got friendly with a doctor who lived in Paradise Pastures – hellish place the other side of Naparima, I expect you know it. I would have said that her life had become rather full rather than otherwise; at least it was too full to make room for me. She went and I stayed, and here I am still.'

'I am sorry to hear it,' said Alfred. He wondered if he could now mention the reason for his visit. He had no desire at all to receive the confidences of strangers, and yet it might seem rather tactless to mention something as banal as delivering a letter in the midst of Mr Barratt recounting his tragic life. He wished he had had the sense to have used the post. But then he had wanted to see Simon.

'This place has a way of holding people,' said Mr Barratt, mistaking his silence for interest. 'You see, I am the manager of Da Silva here. Our business is shot to hell, if you will pardon the expression. Trade is awful, and any trade there is is through Port of Spain anyway. This little enterprise is doomed, and I am doomed with it.'

'Surely not,' said Alfred. 'I mean, Da Silva is a huge firm.'

'Da Silva will be all right; it is only Da Silva in San Fernando that won't be. They'll shut this place down before long. The lease, you see, runs out in a couple of months and it won't be renewed.'

'How do you know that?' asked Alfred a little sharply.

'I know,' said Mr Barratt with a look of great meaning. He glanced at his watch. It was only 8.35. 'I suppose I could tell you the truth in the strictest confidence. Perhaps we could have a little drink. I find it often helps me to get my mind in order.'

'Yes, yes, I'd like to know,' said Alfred. He was curious and wanted to know what would happen to Simon. This seemed to be the best opportunity to find out, and he resolved to overcome his dislike of conversation with strangers.

Mr Barratt was unlocking his desk and taking out a bottle of whisky.

'I am afraid that there is only one glass,' he said.

27

'You go ahead,' said Alfred, relieved. 'I don't mind at all.'

Barratt poured himself some whisky with great care, as if it were medicine. He took a hesitant sip, and then began to speak.

'I suppose you know all about a character called Seth,' he said.

'I don't think so,' said Alfred.

Barratt looked at him with a renewed interest. It occurred to him that for the first time in his life he was speaking to an innocent.

'Mr Seth,' said Barratt, 'is the most important man in San Fernando. I have never met him. He lives up Naparima Hill, beyond your own house, in fact. You carry on up the road until it becomes little more than a dirt track. You reach a high wall with a solid metal gate and behind that is where the mysterious Mr Seth lives. He is something of a recluse. They say his parents were poor people and that he is a self-made man. Perhaps he is so very retiring out of modesty. But the fact is that he has bought the freehold of this building. Most of the town is on leasehold, you know, just like London, and he has bought up all the leases without anyone really noticing. He has some dummy company that has bought up the entire waterfront, including our offices and our jetty, and very soon most of these leases will expire.'

'But why would this Mr Seth want to own most of San Fernando? It can't be any use to him. Surely he will lease the place back to you?'

'That is what you or I or any sensible person would say,' agreed Barratt. 'But Seth may have some crazy idea of making his fortune in property speculation. He is worth a fortune as it is. But they say that people with money always want more of it.'

Barratt fell silent and poured himself some more whisky. Alfred feared that the man would soon be too drunk to make sense, and that he had better steer the conversation in the direction he required before it was too late.

'Mr Barratt,' he said, leaning forward. 'There is a young man called Simon Palmer who works here. If this Mr Seth is not going to renew your lease as you seem to imply, and Da Silva gives up its operation here as a result, what will happen to him? I'm only

28

asking because the young man is a friend of Archbishop Nourganian and I feel a little responsible for him.'

Barratt took a gulp of whisky. His own employment prospects when the lease ran out were practically nil. Alcohol-induced melancholy had led him to conclude this, and his present frame of mind coloured the opinion he gave of Simon's prospects as well.

'When the lease runs out, so will Palmer's job,' he said shortly. 'Da Silva will just get rid of us all.'

'And when does the lease run out?'

'In February.'

'Well, I must wish you good morning, Mr Barratt,' said Alfred, making as to get up. 'I originally came here to leave a message for young Palmer. It is strange to think that I have never heard of this Mr Seth before. I suppose that he isn't a Catholic. His name doesn't sound very Catholic to me.'

'He's either a Muslim or a Hindoo,' said Barratt. 'Or, more likely than that, he is a worshipper of Mammon. Seth has sucked this town dry.'

The Bishop laughed uneasily at this remark. Taking leave of a drunk man was always rather awkward. Barratt had remained seated and glum in front of his whisky glass. Alfred extended his hand and, when Barratt did not take it, he made a rather clumsy gesture with it that was half wave and half benediction. He crept out of the room and shut the door. The door, he now noticed, had the word MANAGER painted on it in peeling black paint.

He was now in the main office and could feel the curious eyes of the clerks upon him. It seemed that a visitor was unusual in this indolent place. He wondered if any one of them were reliable enough to be entrusted with his letter to Simon. He was about to speak when Simon himself appeared.

'I am afraid I was out when you called,' he said apologetically.

'I've just had a most interesting talk with your manager,' said Alfred, aware that the curious eyes were still devouring him. 'But I came to give you this.' He took a crumpled envelope out of his pocket. 'It is to invite you to lunch with me this Sunday. I eat at 12.15 sharp.'

'I'd be delighted,' said Simon.

The young man spoke with great deference. Alfred felt a momentary pain as he realised that he would never know whether he was delighted or not. The young man was a stranger to him. They were divided by an abyss of politeness. He felt ill at ease. It was so difficult to get away from people: he had intended to come into Da Silva simply to deliver an impersonal letter, and yet he had already been forced to hear Mr Barratt's life story and all about a man he had never even heard of, Mr Seth. Once you had heard of people it was impossible to erase them from your mind. Mr Barratt's sister Pat had been an old flame of his long-dead brother Hugo, who had driven his car off a cliff under, it was always presumed, the influence of alcohol. In a crueller world, Mr Barratt might have been his brother-in-law, and his sister Simon's aunt. It was as if a terrible web of connexions closed them in, imprisoning them – and all they could do was be polite to each other, to hold each other at bay.

'You have met our Manager?' Simon was saying, filling in the silence.

'Oh yes, it was most interesting,' said Alfred hopelessly, noting that it was always the opposite of the truth that slipped out the most easily. 'I look forward to seeing you on Sunday,' he added and held out his hand.

A moment later he was outside Da Silva. Even the brightness of the sky could not alleviate the dullness of the brown harbour water, the derelict appearance of the ships or the sorry appearance of the buildings lining the sea-front. He wondered about Mr Seth for a moment, and why he should want the so plainly undesirable; then he turned homeward before the heat of the day should become too intense.

4

IT RAINED that Sunday, which was unusual, as December was supposed to be a dry month. That was why the sacristan of the Cathedral was taken off his guard. All the metal buckets that were used to catch the leaks had been stored away in some inaccessible cubby-hole, and the noise of the first downpour was accompanied by muffled clankings as the poor man fought his way over step-ladders and broken statuary to get hold of them. By the time he had put them in their usual places, under the worst leaks, small pools of rainwater had already formed on the wooden floor. The Bishop's sermon was punctuated by the sharp report of raindrops falling on metal.

It was not a very good sermon; it was rather like one of those sermons at a funeral where the priest is desperate to say something good about the deceased and, in his inability to do so, ends up saying far too much, and straying into the realms of embarrassment. The clinking in the buckets did not help. As Alfred reached the end of his unsatisfactory sermon he at least had the comfort that no one was listening to him, least of all himself.

The reason he was saying Mass publicly in the Cathedral was that the Vicar-General had departed, and the Vicar-General had been the parish priest of the Cathedral parish. The old man had gone rather earlier than Alfred had expected – in fact he had gone as soon as he had been able to, once the Archbishop had told him he was to be replaced. As he had left before his replacement arrived, Alfred was forced to fill the gap. This was not what he wanted: the previous night he had taken the unusual step (for him at least) of telephoning Archbishop Nourganian and asking him to send Father Salvatori down as soon as possible. He had, he now supposed, panicked rather. The Archbishop had been soothing. He said that Salvatori had already left Port of Spain and was on his way. Alfred felt profoundly grateful and said so. It was then that Nourganian, still in the most soothing tones, had slipped in his master-stroke: Salvatori, he said, would move into the Bishop's House by tomorrow night. This was a new development: until now the Vicar-General had lived next to the Cathedral. But Alfred found it impossible to protest. He just said that he was grateful for the man's arrival. He had been caught out.

He celebrated Mass that morning with a sense of resentment caused by the thought of the imminent arrival of the stranger. He shuddered to think of having him in his house. Alphonsus Nourganian had been very clever indeed. If he wanted to force Alfred into resignation, this was the way to go about it. Perhaps Salvatori was so obnoxious that he would be forced to leave San Fernando just to get away from him. He imagined a ghastly war of domestic attrition. They would have to share a bathroom. As he elevated the Sacred Host, he realised that he had not shared a bathroom with anyone since his youth. He wondered whether it were possible actually to like anyone one had to share a bathroom with. As he pronounced the words of consecration over the chalice, he reflected that he knew absolutely nothing about the man, nor had he bothered to ask anything about him. And he had Simon Palmer coming to luncheon that very day. It was too much to contend with.

Depression settled on him in the silence after Holy Communion. Here he was, in his own Cathedral, yet there was no place on earth that he could call his own. The Cathedral was invaded by rain, and even his own house was being invaded by a stranger. Perhaps help would come from somewhere. 'My help shall come from the Lord, who made heaven and earth,' he said to himself. They said that God could transform everything, however hopeless it seemed. This grain of comfort was accompanied by the sneaking realisation that when the really torrential rains came in a few months' time the entire Cathedral roof might collapse under their violence. He stood up to finish the Mass, unable to bear the thought any longer.

A few moments later he was struggling up the hill with a borrowed umbrella. To his relief no one had arrived in his absence. It was only ten in the morning. Salvatori would surely not arrive until the evening; if he had meant to be there for lunch he would have let that be known.

Alfred went into his silent sitting-room. All was the same: the hard unwelcoming chairs, the polished floor, the bare walls and the shuttered doors that led out onto the verandah. He opened them and stepped out to look at the rain, now drizzling to a halt. The town below him seemed fresh after rainfall, and even the sea was unnaturally smooth and glassy. His habitual view was now almost picturesque. Somewhere down there Simon Palmer was bound to live. He had no view in the opposite direction, up Naparima Hill, or towards Paradise Pastures. In that direction lay Mr Seth. Only yesterday he had walked up the road, drawn by curiosity, to look at the high wall and its metal gate, wondering why he had never noticed them before.

With all the abruptness of West Indian weather, the rain had stopped and been replaced by the brightening sun. He retreated indoors and shut out the light. He went into the hallway and stood by the table on which was a supply of scraps of paper. He wrote: 'Rum, limes, sugar and Angosturas to the dining-room please.' Then he rang the little bell that stood on the table. He returned to the sitting-room, and soon he heard his housekeeper's footsteps; a few moments later he heard her putting the things he had requested in the dining-room. When the faceless servant was out of the way, he went in and made the rum punch.

He had said Mass three times that day – at seven, at eight and at nine o'clock. Even on a Sunday everything started early to avoid the heat. There were about thirty-thousand people in San Fernando. Half were probably Muslims or Hindoos, he thought; the other half were Christians, of which about half again were probably Catholics. That made seven and a half thousand. This was a disquieting statistic, for at the three Masses there had not been more than a thousand present at most. And the roof leaked. There would be plenty for John Salvatori to do. He would be kept so busy doing up the Cathedral and winning back the lapsed that he would hardly ever be in the house. This was a cheerful thought, the first he had had all day.

Thus cheered, he went back into the sitting-room. He crossed the room to a small roll-topped desk, which he unlocked. He searched until he found a type-written letter that he had received some months before but not paid much attention to at the time. It was from his brother-in-law, a financial man in London, who looked after the Palmer-Ross money. Part of this money was Alfred's. He had inherited a considerable amount from his parents, and it had been cultivated on his behalf since then. As he had never cause to spend any money, his portfolio was never depleted, and the investments had continued to grow undisturbed. The letter he had spoke of stocks and shares in companies he had never heard of; various figures were mentioned, in pounds sterling, not American or Trinidad-and-Tobago dollars. Because this was so, and because Alfred had only a hazy idea of the current exchange rates, this rather blunted the impact of the figures; but even so he could see that if he wanted to repair the Cathedral out of his own pocket he could well afford to do so. There were other things he could do with the money too. Years ago, when his brother Hugo had killed himself in a car crash and he had inherited his share of Hugo's estate, he had given it all away to various charities. Perhaps the time to spend would come again. The last time it had been the College in Port of Spain that had benefited, the place where Simon had been educated.

*

At noon the bell rang and he went to answer it himself. He managed the brightest smile he could at the sight of the boy, and immediately told himself not to think of him as a boy – no one of twenty-seven could be thought of as a child. And yet the word 'boy' always came into his mind in connexion with Simon, for he had never seen him

34

as a child, and could not quite get used to the idea of all those lost years.

They stood on the verandah.

'Show me where you live,' said Alfred.

'Somewhere over there,' he said, pointing. 'A little to the right of the Cathedral. I was there at the eight o'clock Mass, but perhaps you did not see me.'

'I don't look at the congregation much,' admitted Alfred. 'I am not like Archbishop Alphonsus or Father Salvatori.'

'Yes,' said Simon. 'Father Salvatori is certainly very apostolic, isn't he? I knew him in Port of Spain, though only very slightly.'

'He is coming here. He will be parish priest and Vicar-General of the diocese. Do you think he will like San Fernando?'

'Not much,' said Simon, contemplating the view. 'It can't really compare with Port of Spain. There's no Savannah, no racing, nothing much of interest. I only came here because they sent me and I thought it would do my career good.'

'And how could it help your career?' asked Alfred gently. 'You will have to explain it all to me.'

'Well, it is a small operation here, and the business has become stagnant. None of the clerks do anything all day. What little that gets done gets done in spite of them, not because of them. And Mr Barratt ...'

'Yes, I have met Mr Barratt.'

'They told me in Port of Spain that Mr Barratt had rather given up. The poor man has never really recovered from his wife's leaving him, they say. He's often very depressed and not up to much work as a result. The truth is that all those clerks should be given the push, as they are just a dead weight. But he hasn't had the energy to do anything about it, so the whole of Da Silva's has gone into a decline. That is why there is an opportunity for me, if I can get the whole thing to work again. Then after a year or two I could go back to Port of Spain and have a much better job in the office there. If I hadn't come here I'd have been stuck behind the same desk for the rest of my life. Eight years were enough.'

'Eight years,' repeated Alfred, trying to imagine eight years chained to the same desk, and failing to do so. 'Wouldn't you have preferred to have gone to University?' he inquired innocently.

'Oh yes. But my mother wanted me to get a job as soon as I left school. She wasn't particularly well at the time and she wasn't able to work as hard as she did in the past. When I asked the Archbishop about what to do, he told me that I should support my mother, as there was no one else who would.'

'It was very generous of you to do so,' said Alfred, suppressing a spasm of annoyance with the Archbishop. 'Perhaps one day the loss will be made good.'

'I used to wonder about what it would have been like,' said Simon. 'I don't any more. What you have never known you cannot miss. At least that is what they say; I sometimes think that you can. Sometimes you feel that you have some destiny that you have not yet discovered. I used to think that I ought to be a priest.'

'Used to?' said Alfred hesitantly.

'I couldn't really see myself as a priest,' he said. 'People like Father John Salvatori look like priests, so much so that you can't imagine them ever having been anything else. They are born that way; I didn't quite know what way I had been born, what I was meant to be.'

The tinkling bell sounded.

'That means that we must go in for luncheon,' said Alfred.

After he had said the grace over the food, he asked Simon about the nature of his work at Da Silva. The question of the lease came up immediately.

'I've got to get Mr Barratt to try and renegotiate our lease. For some reason he won't do it. He says he has tried and failed, and that he won't try again. But I think he has given up too easily. Mr Seth just wants us to pay a higher rent, that's all. There's no one else who would want our offices, I'm sure of that. If we have to move out, there's no one else who would move in.'

'And can't Da Silva move its office to somewhere else?'

'It can't. Mr Seth seems to have bought up every lease in the town. And I think the people in Port of Spain think that its hardly worth the trouble.'

'I can't for the life of me see why anyone would want to spend so much money buying up the whole of San Fernando,' said Alfred in genuine puzzlement. 'It is quite ridiculous.'

'That is what I think too. That is why it must just be a ploy to try and force up the rent. So many leases are expiring about now ...'

'Poor Mr Barratt,' said Alfred, taking a sip from his glass. 'I don't envy him at all; these people will always try and drive hard bargains.'

'Rich people always want more,' said Simon, who thought Seth's wealth his distinguishing characteristic; the Bishop, though, had been thinking of Seth's race.

'Are poor people content with less?' said Alfred. 'You must have some ambitions?'

'I'd like to get married one day,' he said, 'when I get back to Port of Spain, when I have got some money to live on. But really all my ambitions are rather vague.'

Alfred thought of all his stocks and shares in London. How useless they were to him; and they were also useless to Simon. For how could he say 'Don't worry about money ever again. I'll pay for everything you want'? It might seem an appealing idea, but the fact remained that you simply could not endow a relative stranger with a fortune, especially when you had only met him three times. It could not be done. The dangerous thought occurred to him that perhaps he should simply blurt out the truth, tell him that he was his father. But that would be worse than fatal; for while it was true that he was his father, it was equally true that he had neglected him for twenty-seven years. The truth was never simple; to tell the truth here would ruin everything.

You could not make bricks without straw, Alfred thought to himself. The boy wanted to marry and settle down in Port of Spain, and work modestly for Da Silva. He took after his mother. The culture of submission ran in his blood, reinforced by his upbringing. He wasn't like a Palmer-Ross, and couldn't be made into one. Alfred knew that the Palmer-Rosses were appalling snobs. It was one of their good points. They could never bear to submit to being second to anyone. They always pushed themselves to be first; strangers might say that they had high standards of excellence. He remembered how his mother had despised all the people her children had married. She had sniffily mentioned the word 'degeneracy'. There had been a sort of familial racism about her: she saw her own family as a master race. Alfred had thought this one of her more eccentric attitudes; but now, as he looked at Simon, who was a very fine-looking young man, he regretted that he did not have something of his paternal grandmother's spirit. She would never have put up with Mr Barratt. He realised now that his poor dead brother Hugo, who had been her favourite, would never have dared tell her about any liking he might have had for Barratt's sister. It would have made her furious.

'One of my brothers used to go around with Mr Barratt's sister,' he said aloud. 'His name was Hugo, and he's been dead for years, but all the same, all our families seem to be connected somehow.'

'I've noticed how everyone is related to everyone else in Trinidad,' said Simon. 'But I haven't got any relatives at all. My mother had brothers and sisters, but she never saw them and hardly ever mentioned them.'

'You have a sort of adopted family, though,' said Alfred. 'The Church – and Archbishop Nourganian in particular.'

'Yes,' said Simon and was silent a moment, before saying: 'And I shall be glad to see Father Salvatori when he arrives.'

'I expect him to get here tonight.'

*

Simon remembered Father Salvatori well; and the truth was that Father Salvatori had the gift of making people remember him, even when they had only met him once. (Twice or thrice and they were his for life.) To the innocent Simon, there had been something so

38

kind in Father Salvatori's aspect that he had thought it comparable to the effect that saints were supposed to have on everyone they met. At various times in the past admirers of the Father had compared him to Saint Francis for gentleness and Leo the Great for his personal magnetism. He was thought to be the sort of man who could do anything, so persuasive was he: he could have dealt with Attila the Hun's unwelcome arrival, or charmed the Wolf of Gubbio into domestication.

Father Salvatori had that sort of smile that many called ingratiating; but for those who were well-disposed towards the clergy – no matter how little the clergy returned their regard – for such as these, his smile was angelic. He himself knew this quite well; and he also knew that angels are pure spirit and have no bodies; that what has no body has no face; and what has no face cannot smile. Thus angelic smiles were nonsense. However, he was quite prepared to tolerate this sort of nonsense when it flattered him. Simon Palmer was not to know this, but Father Salvatori, like many holy men, had one secret vice that he cultivated in the mistaken belief that it was harmless. This innocent vice was vanity. It was something that Simon would never have recognised as he had never experienced it.

Father Salvatori's vanity was in some ways similar to that type of vanity usually associated with beautiful women. He took great care over his appearance. He was always well-dressed, which was something of an achievement in the tropics. He never appeared to be worse for the heat, and his clothes conveyed an inner coolness about them. He wore white clerical shirts that were exquisitely laundered, white and shining like his teeth. A neat hair-cut showed off his Pre-Raphaelite golden-coloured hair to great advantage. When he smiled one of his famous smiles, his cheeks dimpled. He avoided the sun as much as he could, being very much a man for indoors, and his skin did not resemble chamois leather as a result. Were it not for the fact that he was a priest and approaching forty, he might have been taken for a virginal teenager, rather than a saint.

This personal vanity was not vanity at all as far as he was

concerned, but rather sprang from a sincere desire to propagate the Catholic religion. A good priest had to be of good appearance, and an unkempt clergyman might well put a soul off eternal salvation.

As a priest in Port of Spain he had been very successful, and chiefly among women of a certain age and class. If there had been such a thing as Society in Trinidad, he would have been its natural chaplain. In all the best houses in Maraval and Cascade, his name was mentioned with something approaching reverence. He attracted modest crowds, but crowds nevertheless, when he preached, and though very few might profess to understand these sermons, they were widely praised for their delivery. In fact, John Salvatori had something of a following, and the Archbishop, who was old enough to remember, thought he was rather similar to what Alfred Palmer-Ross had been at the same age. There was the same social smoothness, except that in Alfred's case the smoothness had been natural. He had been born with it; John Salvatori had had to learn it, which, in a strange way, was an advantage, as it meant that he was ever eager to please. Alfred had never been that.

Apart from this, Salvatori had distinguished himself in more solid ways. He had been the Archbishop's secretary. Despite his smoothness, he had shown that he could organise things. To the septuagenarian mind of Nourganian, behind every act of organisation lay a certain ruthlessness. It was this last quality, he thought, that would make him an excellent Vicar-General in San Fernando.

*

'I suppose,' said Alfred, his mind on Salvatori, 'I suppose he must be a wondrous necessary man.'

He said this as lunch drew to a close.

'What is a wondrous necessary man?' asked Simon.

'It is a type. The phrase comes from Shakespeare. I suppose there is some modern equivalent. It means someone who makes himself indispensable to everyone. I can hardly believe that Alphonsus can bring himself to part with him.'

'Yes,' said Simon. 'He is a man who is very much to be liked.'

*

The truth of this became apparent that very evening after Simon had left. Darkness fell quickly, as it always did, without warning. Some ten minutes before sunset, the doorbell rang. Alfred heard it as he paced the verandah at the back of the house, reciting his breviary. He waited until he had finished the Divine Office and then stepped into the twilit hall. John Salvatori stood before him, like some child awaiting his headmaster, a little uncertainly. Alfred put out his hand. Soft lips touched it in the darkness as the blond head leaned over it. Alfred managed to say a few words of welcome. The head was raised, and even the gathering darkness could not dim that radiant smile. This indeed, Alfred realised, was a man very much to be liked.

5

BREAKFAST TIME had never been the best of times with Mr Barratt. Even as a youth getting out of bed had always been something of a struggle. With early married life, incentives to get up had arrived; he had a family to support – or rather should have had. The departure of Mrs Barratt had brought a return to old ways. He now had hardly any reason to get up at all.

He hated his job with Da Silva; yet he lived in perpetual fear of being given the sack. He knew that this was illogical, but he felt that his enslavement to Da Silva was the only thing that tied him down to what might be described as real life. Beyond the office there was only a blank, or a nightmare landscape, induced by alcoholic excess. Hence the difficulty he experienced every morning: he had to go to Da Silva, even though he hated it, as it was the only thing that stopped him being utterly inebriated all the time. However, he always needed a beer or two to help him face getting out of bed to go there.

Like everyone else in San Fernando he woke at six; he lived next door to the Chief of Police, whose Alsatian began its lonely barking at that hour. But Mr Barrat, unlike everyone else, would lie in bed for an hour and not get up until seven. This hour of sipping Heineken was the time of day in which the spirit of alcohol might try and drive away the other demons that threatened him. Chief of these was his departed wife. He had no real idea of where she was now, nor of how her new life with the doctor from Paradise Pastures was progressing. He had no clear idea of what she would be like either, after so long an interval. This very imprecision gave his mind full freedom in its imagination. Perhaps she was radiantly happy and still beautiful, but there again perhaps she wasn't. He wasn't sure which would please him most. Hers was a strange existence in his mind. Sometimes he wondered if she was in fact dead; he had even got so far as to think of whom he could ask, who would know whether she was alive or dead. But something always held him back. The real woman he had been married to no longer existed; what disturbed him was purely something within the confines of his own mind – whether she was alive or not was irrelevant; even certain knowledge of her death would not free his mind of her.

Recently a new demon had appeared to plague him. This was a man he had never met, Mr Seth. Sometimes he thought of Mr Seth with despair, and sometimes with wild hopes. In Mr Seth's hands lay the future of Da Silva in San Fernando. He could renew the lease or he could end it. He had the power of life or death over Mr Barratt and his career. For if Da Silva were to fold, Mr Barratt would be what he most feared, a free man. Thus Mr Seth was like a kindly gaoler to him, who, if he were kind enough, might just let him live on in the prison and not cast him out into the world to fend for himself. Surely he could not be so cruel.

He had written to him and received hopeless, uncompromising answers. He had allowed himself to despair. But now, on Monday morning, after the second beer, hope stirred afresh. Perhaps, he thought again, a personal interview might help. He could go to the house at the top of the hill. The door had not been utterly closed. Mr Seth had never said that the renewal of the lease was utterly out of the question. Perhaps Mr Seth was being so hard because he wanted him to come up and see him, and beg if necessary. If that were the case, he would do it. And with this sudden resolution, he heaved himself out of bed.

That salutary time in front of the shaving-mirror dented his new-found confidence. The bloodshot eyes and the yellowing skin were hardly the things to inspire trust in himself or Mr Seth, he feared. The walk to the office and the daily sights of the ramshackle town merely reinforced this impression. Even the sight of Da Silva itself made him think that perhaps Mr Seth's

43

ambition to close the place down was a piece of well-planned euthanasia.

By ten o'clock any thought of going up the hill to see Mr Seth had vanished, along with half a bottle of whisky which he had thought might restore his determination. The blackest despair was only averted by the entry of Simon Palmer. It suddenly entered his mind that this was the solution: he could send young Palmer, an innocent, into the lions' den, where he himself so feared to go.

'Go and speak to Mr Seth,' said Barratt. 'Informally, I mean. Try and find out what he really wants. Go up and see if he's at home.'

He noticed that the young man hesitated.

'He may tell you things that he would never tell me,' explained Barratt, who sometimes saw himself as the victim of Mr Seth's racial prejudice.

*

So Simon set off up the hill.

The man he was going to see lived behind a high concrete wall, pierced by a solid metal gate. Those who wished to enter had to use an intercom. Simon stated his business and name, his face was scrutinised by a camera, and after a pause the gate swung open with a loud buzz and click. He was surprised at how easy it was to gain entry. It was almost as if he had been expected.

From bright sunlight reflected off concrete, he stepped into a world of shade. He was in a garden, under a canopy of trees, and a man was speaking to him. But this was not so: the man was looking at him and speaking about him into a telephone; he was sitting in a small cabin, and staring at him through the glass window. This was a little unsettling, as it reminded him of films he had seen about people crossing borders, being interviewed by hostile and faceless armed guards. The man in the sentry box was more than a gardener. But before Simon could determine whether he was armed or not, he was leaving the cabin and gesturing him to follow.

They walked through the shady part of the garden along a concrete path to what he assumed was the back door of the house. Through a louvred window he glimpsed two corpulent maids sitting motionless as statues in a silent kitchen. Soon they were in a dark corridor, air-conditioned into coldness.

His guide eventually arrived at a door and knocked at it; then, without waiting for a reply, he opened it and almost pushed Simon inside. Simon found himself in the presence of Mr Seth. The room was dark, and he could discern an old man with a balding head.

'I am sorry to have kept you waiting,' said Mr Seth pleasantly. 'Do sit down. Friends of mine have spoken to me about you, and I was just telephoning them to see if you had in fact left your office. One has to be so careful these days when someone one doesn't know calls on one. I hope the air-conditioning here isn't too cold for you? I find it a great help myself – indeed I hardly leave the house these days, I have got so used to it. Perhaps you are not? I think I saw you shiver?'

This last question seemed to demand an answer.

'I am not used to air-conditioning,' lied Simon politely.

'Some people find it a little off-putting,' said Mr Seth quietly. 'I dare say that my habits are rather strange; I can barely bear to see the sunlight; as I say, I hardly ever go out, and very few people ever come to see me. I have been rather reclusive ever since I lost my eye. Do you see why?'

Simon, now that his eyes were accustomed to the lack of light, could see only too well. Mr Seth had only one eye; the cheek and the eyebrow above the empty socket were bisected by a large scar. It was the sight of this, in the dark cold room, that had made him shiver.

'I rely heavily on my two boys,' continued Mr Seth. 'One of them showed you in. When you go, doubtless you will ask them how I came to lose my eye. They will be only too happy to tell you the story. It is a story they have been brought up on, and they love telling it. Most people find it very instructive.'

'I have been sent here –' began Simon.

'Yes, yes, yes,' said Seth a little impatiently. 'That tiresome Barratt. I know what he wants from me. I am surprised that a bright young man like you should work for him.'

'But I work for Da Silva –'

'I feel,' said Mr Seth, 'that Barratt is not quite reliable. Whenever he has spoken to me on the telephone, I have found his speech a little laboured. He drinks and he talks far too much, and I think he has been there far too long. I have no prejudice against Da Silva. Such a reputable firm. In the import export trade there is no firm that I would rather work with ...'

'Do you have something in mind?' asked Simon, remembering that he was supposed to try and find out what the man really wanted.

Mr Seth fell into a muse. 'Do you know much about my business?' he asked.

'I know nothing at all.'

'They tell me that you have just arrived here from Port of Spain. Then you do not know that San Fernando is a dying town. The proof of that is that I have been able to buy up most of the commercial properties here with ease, and cheaply too. Yet cheap isn't cheap enough. Most of the business in Trinidad now goes on in Port of Spain. San Fernando is dying, and any property here is almost worthless. But if the place could be brought to life again ... do you see? Trade is my interest. Venezuela and Colombia are so close; there are so many opportunities; we are so close to the United States too. But is Mr Barratt the man to use these opportunities? Could he be useful to me?'

Simon was silent. He knew that Mr Barratt was not a useful man in this context. Any work that was done at Da Silva was done by Simon, not by Mr Barratt, but to admit this would be disloyal. Even to continue in silence could be interpreted as disloyalty.

'Mr Barratt will always be manager of Da Silva,' he said, more bluntly than he had intended to.

'I am afraid that is true,' said Seth regretfully. 'Da Silva will never sack anyone for laziness or incompetence, especially not a white man, as those are supposed to be the faults of black men. Isn't that what they say? The white man's burden?'

Simon knew that this was true, but again kept silent, unwilling to be drawn into a conspiracy of agreement with Seth.

'If you were white, Mr Palmer,' continued Seth remorselessly, 'wouldn't you be the manager of Da Silva? You are manager in all but name already.'

'How do you know that?' asked Simon.

'My boys tell me things. They go down to the town every now and then, and that's when they meet up with the boys who work for you. They say that before you came here they sat on their asses all day, but now they have to work, at least when you are looking. Good. There are too many people in this country who sit on their asses and expect other people to pay for it. I got rich through sweat and blood, and I don't admire people who don't work. My boys know that and they respect me for it. I can use men who work, men like you, but I can't use men like your Mr Barratt.'

'But Mr Barratt is not going to resign,' said Simon, trying to bring the conversation back to practicalities.

'And that is the pity of it,' said Seth. 'But the question is this: do you want to get on, and do you want Barratt's job?'

'I – would prefer to go back to Port of Spain,' said Simon, which was the truth, though he had been made uncomfortable by what Seth had said, and wondered if the old man had not read his character too well. It was a shock to think that there were clerks in the office who were watching him and reporting every-thing back to Seth. It made him frightened to think that he had been observed so long, for he feared that Seth might now know all sorts of things about him, and this would put him in the man's power.

'If you go back to Port of Spain,' Seth was saying, 'you will end up like all those other men who work for Da Silva, all those bright boys who never had families to help them. You will get nowhere.'

'I don't know why I should be of such interest to you,' said Simon coldly, but knowing that there was truth in what the man said.

'I want to help you. I am interested in you and I know about you. I would be very pleased to see you manage Da Silva. It would provide an outlet for my various interests. I have an idea to write to the head office of Da Silva and tell them that I will renew the lease in perpetuity on one condition, provided that they make you manager.'

'Please don't do it,' said Simon in hurried tones. 'It would do me no end of harm; they would think that I had put you up to it; and I really don't want to owe my promotion to anyone.'

'You wouldn't be in my debt, I would be in yours,' said Seth quietly. 'We will talk about this again. Our little talk has lasted some time. But I feel I can't let you go just yet. It is nearly time for something to eat. I am sure you are in no hurry to get back. My boys will entertain you. I insist on it.'

Mr Seth pressed a little buzzer, and in came the 'boy' that Simon had seen before.

'I will see you again soon,' said Mr Seth. 'Now go with Burke.'

Burke was the man's name; he led Simon out into the corridor and shut the door behind them. 'You want sit by the pool?' he enquired.

'I really have to get back –'

'After lunch,' said Burke, a man not accustomed to listening to reason. 'Right now you are going to sit by the pool and enjoy yourself. That is what the Boss says.'

He was led away towards a side of the house he had not seen until now, out into the garden, which was hot and bright after the cold claustrophobia of the house. There was a swimming-pool there, fresh and inviting on the warm December day. By it stood a large canopied seat, into which he was guided by Burke. Another of Mr Seth's boys appeared, who looked at him with dull uncomprehending eyes, and uttered only one word: 'Smoke?'

Simon nodded. Co-operation seemed to be the wisest course. There was something brutal about these two men; he watched the nameless one rolling a cigarette. Both he and Burke were very large and strong, and very black. They both seemed to cultivate silent dispositions that were calculated to make people nervous of them. Simon felt that either of them might fly into a rage without the slightest warning and with the merest provocation. Either could easily kill him with his bare hands, if the idea entered his dull head to do so; and who was to know if they did decide to kill him?

He took the cigarette when it was ready, accepted a light, and began to smoke it. You did hear stories about how condemned men were allowed one last cigarette – but perhaps they were not out to kill him after all, for they would probably have done so by now, if that was what they had decided to do. Simon did not usually smoke, but he felt a sense of relaxation creep over him under the influence of the cigarette.

'How did Mr Seth lose his eye?' he asked boldly, suddenly remembering what he had been told to ask.

Burke gave a low laugh, to show that this was the question he had been waiting for.

'He lost his eye,' he said, 'when Tony Singh pulled it out in a fight.'

Simon wondered who Tony Singh was. He felt he was expected to know, for Burke seemed to sense that this revelation had not had the desired effect.

'Tony Singh,' Burke began again, making a second attempt, 'was a mighty man who ended up in a fishing net. Some fishermen found his corpse, and no one ever found out who did it, least of all the police. But they didn't ask many questions, even though some of us could have been able to tell them a lot, but Tony Singh wasn't popular with the police, and they were only too glad to have him out of the way.'

'I see,' said Simon. He tried to get it clear in his mind, for his mind felt rather fuzzy under the influence of what was in fact not tobacco but ganga. Tony Singh had pulled out Seth's eye and

Seth had murdered Tony Singh in return, and the police had done nothing. This was Seth's claim to fame, and it was this violent past that had won him so much respect in San Fernando, a place where murderers were heroes.

Simon took another pull on his cigarette. 'Mr Seth is a rich man,' he said.

'He pays us well,' said the other man, Burke's companion, and to judge by his appearance, his brother as well. 'He's very good to us.'

These words were enunciated with great effort and very slowly.

The two fat maids appeared and began to prepare a table for lunch. Simon was offered whisky but, conscious of a swimming head, refused it. Then, as they began to eat by the pool-side, almost on cue, a girl in a bikini appeared from the house. But Burke shouted something at her – possibly her name – and she scuttled away.

'This business is no business for a woman,' he said by way of explanation, noting how Simon's eyes had followed the girl. 'You'll see her again if you become a partner of ours.'

The rest of the meal passed in oppressive silence. Once it was over, Simon was shown to the same door by which he had entered.

'Mr Seth will be waiting for your next visit,' he was warned as he left.

6

CLIMBING OVER roofs had never really appealed to John Salvatori, but that very morning, while Simon was at Mr Seth's, he did climb up to inspect the Cathedral roof at close hand. To climb over it was quite impossible, as it seemed clear enough that it could not hold his weight. This experience of dilapidation at first hand was slightly depressing. It had the opposite effect on the aged sacristan, who told him that no one had been at all interested in the state of the building for at least fifteen years.

John returned to lunch at the Bishop's house somewhat down-hearted. Only a few days before he had been deep in the counsels of Archbishop Nourganian, and spending his spare time working out complicated cases of canon law in the diocesan marriage tribunal. Now that he was promoted to being a Vicar-General, this new dignity meant that he was forced to worry about leaking roofs, the result of other people's neglect. He wondered if he would get to like Alfred Palmer-Ross. He supposed that he ought to. Domestic harmony always helped, and he had nothing to lose by it. However, the prospect of getting friendly with the Bishop was a tedious one, as Alfred Palmer-Ross had already signified that relations between them were to be formal in the extreme. Breakfast had had to be endured in a frigid silence as the Bishop had said that he never spoke at table.

John's heart sank further when he discovered that luncheon, as his superior called it, was to be as uncomfortable as breakfast. Instead of conversation there was to be reading. The book in question was the *Imitation of Christ* in an archaic translation: while the Bishop ate, John was to read to him, and when the Bishop finished eating the arrangement was reversed. Their voices echoed in the bare room, accompanied by the clink of cutlery. As soon as the food had disappeared, the Bishop stood up to say grace, and then left the room. John dared not follow him onto the verandah.

Instead of disturbing the episcopal solitude, he went out onto the patch of scrub that passed for a garden at the front of the house, and wondered if he might smoke without giving public scandal. There seemed to be no one around. He dared not try to smoke indoors. It might upset the Bishop. All this was very strange: he saw various territorial zones developing in the house, a sort of complicated territorial compromise. Perhaps he should stride out onto the cool verandah at once and stake his claim, lest it be immediately established as the Bishop's sacred and inviolate patch. He lit another cigarette and pondered on his position. (There was still no one around in the hot midday – and like a lot of men who rely on physical charm, he did not like to advertise his imperfections, and smoking was one of them.)

He made up his mind there and then that he would rebuild the Cathedral. He would have the old building demolished and build a completely new one. No one in Trinidad had done that for years: it would make his name. He would get the whole population involved and confirm his reputation as a man of the people. Until now perhaps he had been too much a man for the rich; but no one would be able to say that once he had built a new Cathedral in San Fernando. He would take two or three years over it and then he would be made a Bishop. He would be a Bishop before he was forty, a Bishop somewhere other than this. This was a pleasant prospect indeed. It might be hard work, but it would give him something to do, and if you were to escape from a hole like San Fernando, then you had to work your passage. It was remarkable that he had only been in the place for a day and already he was finding it oppressive. If the Bishop chose to ignore him, even that could be useful, as it would mean that he would be utterly free to get on with his own thing.

He was about to go back into the house, to start ferreting around in the diocesan records, and start his great work at once, when he saw Simon Palmer coming down the road. The ability never to forget a face was something he was proud of. He called to him, and Simon was pleased to be recognised. He explained that he was walking down to his office in the town and that he was late. John Salvatori offered to accompany him.

'You will hate this place, Father,' he said confidentially, when he was asked how he was enjoying San Fernando.

'Have you taken against it so very quickly, then?'

'Everything that is wrong with the West Indies can be found here, magnified,' said Simon.

'You mean the cricket team?'

'Oh no, no. I mean our whole way of life. You know what I mean; everyone knows that dishonesty is in the blood; it's the only way of making a living. Look at the governments we've had. Did you hear about somewhere to the north of here, where the whole government were arrested at Miami Airport for drug smuggling – all three of them?'

'I remember,' said John. 'The British Government had to suspend the Constitution. Even the opposition were dealing in cocaine. But Trinidad is an independent country ...'

'And what about the Professor's daughter?' asked Simon angrily. 'They say that she's the tenth richest woman in the world.'

The Professor had been the previous Prime Minister but one, and had died in office. He had left everything to his daughter, and she had migrated with it to Florida.

'They never proved that there had been anything illegal,' said Salvatori cautiously.

'You don't need proof,' said Simon. 'You just have to look around you. Look at San Fernando. No one does an honest day's work. Our boss is drunk by ten every morning. At least one of our office boys is spying for the man who lives on the hill, who is no better than he ought to be –'

'Is he a rich man?' asked Salvatori innocently.

'He is. He is called Seth and has only got one eye. That much I have seen for myself.' He hesitated, wondering how much he could say without infringing the truth. The whole episode now

53

seemed so strange to him, now that his brain was recovering from the effect of the cigarette he had smoked. 'They say that he is supposed to have put someone out of the way, a man called Tony Singh.'

Much to Simon's surprise Father Salvatori burst into laughter.

'Tony Singh is far more famous now than ever he was when he was alive,' he explained. 'I don't suppose you realise who Tony Singh was. You're far too young. And so am I, but at least I've heard of him. It was some time after the war, and the Chief of the Colonial Police who tried to put Tony Singh away was a Palmer-Ross, some relation of our Bishop, but they never succeeded. Singh was always too clever for them. Then one day they dredged his body out of the sea off Port of Spain. One version of the story has it that he was wearing concrete boots. But let me tell you, Simon, so popular was Tony Singh that lots of people claimed to have murdered him.'

'But you haven't explained who Tony Singh actually was,' said Simon.

'I think I was once told that he ran a gambling den somewhere in Port of Spain. Don't forget that this was before I was born. It started off some sort of gang warfare with the Chinese, who traditionally were supposed to run gambling dens; they must have resented an Indian encroaching on their territory.'

'It all boils down to race eventually,' remarked Simon. 'The Chinese have the laundries and the photography shops and the gambling, the whites have the money and power, the blacks are lazy, while the Indians are full of industriousness.'

'I am surprised at you,' said Father Salvatori, a little taken aback. 'That may have been true once, but Trinidad isn't a colony any more, and things have changed, as I've said before.'

'I wonder if being independent has done us any good at all.'

'I suppose you may be right. They discovered all that oil, and that was supposed to make the country rich but, God alone knows, it all got squandered and stolen. But we live in an imperfect world, and we've got to make the best of what we've got. People know that the people above them are no good, for

54

whatever reason, but it doesn't mean that they don't do their best. We've got to work with the raw material that we find, and we have to realise that some people just won't change. But even if they won't or can't change, remember that all things tend to the glory of God. I think I ought to meet Mr Seth. I suppose he is the richest man in San Fernando?'

'He has got a swimming-pool,' said Simon, almost enviously. 'And he seems to employ at least four people, from what I have seen.'

'Then I must meet him,' said Father Salvatori. 'You can't ignore the most important man in the diocese; and I don't care whether he is a Catholic or not. The thing about the Catholic Church is that everyone ought to belong to it. No one in San Fernando should be exempt from my interference. And as you know him, perhaps you could introduce him to me?'

'Oh but –' said Simon, and was silent. So many thoughts struck him at once that he didn't quite know where to begin his justification for his refusal. That he must justify his refusal cogently and convincingly was very important, for Father John Salvatori – whose blond face was even now smiling at him – was a man to whom it was almost impossible to refuse anything. Simon had known that previously, and he knew it now through personal experience. He could sense from the priest's expectant gaze that he was not accustomed to being refused anything he asked for, especially a simple favour like this. Simon badly felt the need to give in, to say yes, to feel the warm balm of Father Salvatori's approval. He dreaded the other possibility: that that warm smile might grow cold. But – he was frightened of Mr Seth; though he could hardly as yet believe the conversation he had had with the old man, so fantastic did it seem, yet he knew that Mr Seth was old and sinister and had one eye and frightened him. But this hardly seemed an adult manly reason for not wanting to see Mr Seth again. Mr Seth had – possibly or probably, he knew not which – murdered Tony Singh; but Father Salvatori knew this and he wasn't scared of Mr Seth. But it wasn't this distant exploit that he minded, it was Mr Seth himself; Burke and the other man

had also scared him; so had the girl in the bikini, whose frightened face he had but glimpsed – even she unsettled him. He felt
that if he saw them again he might never get away from them,
that he would be sucked into their strange world, where anything
might happen to him.

'I'd rather not see Mr Seth again,' he said weakly, knowing that
his aversion, which had so much of attraction in it, was much
stronger than that, and that if he wanted to see the man again
he had been given an open invitation.

'Why ever not?' asked Father Salvatori, offering him no way
out.

Defeat stared Simon in the face. He was simply not humble
enough to admit to the priest, a man he hardly knew and yet
whose good opinion he already valued, that his was a fear of
temptation and he was not invincible to the blandishments of
Seth.

'You see,' explained the priest, 'I think I am going to need rich
friends to help me rebuild the Cathedral.'

This all-for-a-good-cause line of argument was enough to
make Simon capitulate.

'I can call there whenever I want to, and he never goes out,'
he said.

'Let's go tomorrow afternoon, then,' said Father Salvatori. 'You
can call for me at the Bishop's house on your way up there. One
can't afford to throw away any opportunity, you know. I'll be
expecting you at about two.'

*

Father Salvatori turned and started to make his way back towards
Naparima Hill. Simon watched him go. If the priest had been a more
worldly man, he reflected, he would not have pressed him into
agreeing to take him to Seth's. Simon had the strongest respect for
the clergy, and could not even imagine Father Salvatori understanding, let alone experiencing, the sudden stab of sexual desire
that he had felt a moment ago when recalling to mind the glimpse

of the girl in the bikini. Similarly, he imagined that Father Salvatori did not realise the danger men like Seth posed, unless of course he was making a terrible mistake himself. It could be, he realised, that Mr Seth was a sort of pantomime ogre that no one was scared of apart from Simon Palmer. Suddenly in the bright sunlight of a West Indian afternoon, the whole thing did seem incredible: the two over-sinister bodyguards, the walled and darkened house and the one-eyed monster. After all, it wasn't Mr Seth's fault that he had only one eye; it had upset Simon somewhat to see it, but it wasn't unnatural of itself. Perhaps the unease he felt was a hallucination brought about from smoking that ganga. It could have that effect on you, they said. He would have to see what Mr Barratt said about it. With this in mind, he began to walk back towards Da Silva.

He found Mr Barratt rather sober for the time of day. The poor man had drunk the better part of a bottle of whisky, but the sick excitement he had felt during Simon's absence had nullified the effect of the alcohol.

'Well, Palmer?' he asked as soon as Simon appeared. 'What did he say? I presume you saw him – you have been away long enough.'

'I saw him, sir. He didn't have much to say of interest.'

'Oh. But he must have said something,' ventured Barratt. 'He can't have sat there in silence for two hours and a half.'

'He has got one eye, sir, and he told me that Tony Singh pulled the other out in a fight – and things like that. I think it was his way of trying to tell me that it was best not to interfere with his wishes.'

'Did he say anything about the lease?'

'Not really,' said Simon, gliding over the difficulties of explaining Mr Seth's position.

'What on earth do you mean by "not really"?' asked Mr Barratt, sensing that Simon was hiding something.

'He said that he would never renew the lease while you were manager, sir,' said Simon apologetically.

'I might have known,' said Barratt bitterly. 'I suppose he hates white men, doesn't he?'

Simon was silent. It did seem that Mr Barratt was right on this count. But Simon was far more struck by the fact that in the eyes of Barratt and Seth he was regarded as a black; this was odd, for the clerks in the office, he felt sure, regarded him as more or less white. Perhaps if he were to become manager of Da Silva, everyone would follow their example.

'I did find out one thing, sir,' he said, interrupting his own reflections. 'At least one of the clerks is keeping Seth informed of what is going on down here. He told me so himself; and the proof is that they were expecting me when I arrived. Someone here must have phoned to say I was on my way. And Seth seems to know a great deal about Da Silva.'

'What on earth can we do about that, if we don't know who?' asked Barratt gloomily. 'Of course, I trust you, Palmer, but as for the rest of them, it could be any one of them or all of them. It is one of the things you have to put up with in this bloody country.'

'You could sack them all,' said Simon. 'That would show them that you are not going to be intimidated. And tell them why you are sacking them. Let them tell Mr Seth that you won't put up with this sort of nonsense. Then he'll realise that renewing the lease is in his best interests.'

Mr Barratt seemed suddenly brighter. A way out seemed to be taking shape in his mind.

'If we could convince him we were not going to be black-mailed, then he might do business. But you know, a lot of people would be upset if I sacked those six boys out there.'

'But they're all lazy and they're probably all dishonest,' said Simon.

'Sometimes I think everyone here is,' said Mr Barratt. 'Of course, I know that you are honest, Palmer, for obvious reasons. But you see, if it were only one boy who was being paid by Mr Seth, then the other five would be very resentful. I wouldn't want to risk that. You know how these people can be, don't you?'

'Which people?'

'The blacks,' said Barratt. 'There's no telling what they will do when they have a sense of grievance. And if I were to sack five of them who were innocent, they would have plenty to be sore about. They might come and murder me in my bed tonight.'

Simon realised that Mr Barratt was not the fool he had supposed him to be. He recognised the mechanics of resentment for what they were; he knew how this part of Trinidadian life worked; and in his description of it, Simon recognised part of his own character. There was so much to resent; and once you saw that, you could also see how resentment could shape your entire life. Mr Seth had seen this too.

'I see that,' said Simon, trying to think of the matter in hand and not his own resentments. 'The thing to do is to make it a conditional sacking. Tell them that they will all be sacked unless they tell you who it is who is working for Seth. They must know, as nothing is ever secret, and they'll only too willingly point the finger out of self-interest.'

'Unless they are too frightened of Seth,' said Barratt. 'But we can leave this until tomorrow. Tonight is too late.'

*

Evening fell on San Fernando, as it always did, swiftly, plunging the ill-favoured town into tropical darkness. Mr Barratt made his uncertain way home. At the Bishop's house, Alfred waited for his supper. It was never pleasant to contemplate the passing of another wasted day. He walked around his bare wooden drawing-room, reflecting on the dullness of his life and how the intellectual activities with which he tried to fill it could only fill so much of it. There were gaps. But not everyone's life was so dull. He noted, with something he failed to recognise as envy, that Father Salvatori had seemed to have been busy all day. Then, struck by the awful realisation that there were twenty empty minutes to fill before supper, a time he usually devoted to light reading, and that these twenty minutes were now impossible to fill, so little did he feel like amusing himself with *The Mysterious Affair at Styles* for the umpteenth time – realising this, he rang the bell and, without looking at her, asked the housekeeper to ask Father Salvatori to come down, if he were not too busy.

Father Salvatori came. He came with a smile of catlike satisfaction, recognising his opportunity. He knew he could and would win the Bishop over. His was the way of conciliation, not confrontation, and he had never in his life willingly made an enemy. For him, people existed to be won over.

Alfred was rather flustered by his arrival.

'I just thought,' he began, realising immediately that a complete disclosure of his thoughts would not do; 'I just thought,' he said, 'that you' – it was quite clever to transfer the onus onto him – 'might like to tell me how you passed your first day in San Fernando.'

Alfred felt a wave of relief; his opening sentence had been a success. For this was the first time he had initiated a conversation in years, and he had succeeded in giving nothing away. (He had momentarily forgotten about his conversations with Simon.)

'I visited the Cathedral,' said Salvatori. 'The roof is in rather a bad state.'

'Yes, yes, it is,' agreed Alfred, reassured by these neutral tones. 'Things do get like that in this climate.'

'Indeed. And really, you can't go on repairing wood forever,' continued Salvatori smoothly. 'And so I think it would be a good thing – subject to Your Lordship's permission of course – to rebuild the whole thing from scratch.'

'Rebuild?'

'Build anew, in more durable materials. Concrete would last forever, and it is relatively cheap.'

'And where would you say Mass while the Cathedral was being rebuilt?' asked Alfred.

'I have thought of that. One could build the concrete shell around the old building, and then demolish the old building when the new one was complete; and you could use the wood that hasn't rotted for the doors of the new building.'

'I see that you have got it all worked out,' said Alfred.

A sudden thought struck him: perhaps Father Salvatori had got it into his head that the Bishop would pay for all this extravagance. After all, he supposed that everyone knew that he had inherited money which he had never used till now.

'What about the money?' asked Alfred.

'The local Catholics will pay for it, if I start fund-raising,' said Salvatori. 'They love the idea of building churches, and the bigger the better. This one will be big. We can have a huge campanile, which will serve as a landmark: they love that sort of thing. And then there are bound to be a few very rich people who will fork out: I never underestimate the power of human vanity.'

'Do you mean rich people from Port of Spain?'

'I was thinking of rich people in San Fernando.'

Alfred was impressed by the young man's confidence. He thought of all those dollars: one would have to collect a fair amount before work even started. It would take time.

'Well, it's your Cathedral,' he said. 'Start whenever you want to. What sort of design do you have in mind?'

'A copy of one of the Roman Churches would be best – simplified of course, perhaps something with a dome.'

'Like the Gesu or San Andrea della Valle?'

'Something along those lines. If we copy an existing church, we won't have to spend a fortune employing an architect.'

'It seems that there is no limit to your ambitions. I am glad. Perhaps you will enjoy your time here after all.'

'I hope so,' said Salvatori.

'Ambition is necessary for success,' said Alfred thoughtfully. 'Did you enjoy your time studying in Rome?' he asked, changing the subject, for the whole question of clerical ambition was one that worried him rather.

Priests, as Alfred well knew, were divided on the subject of Rome. They were divided on many things, but when it came to Rome the division was a telling one. Some loathed the place; others loved it. Very few were ever indifferent. As a general rule, those who had not been educated there hated it, often because they were assumed by those who had to be envious of them. (The attribution of the worst motives to their colleagues was a distinguishing mark of the Roman-educated clergy.) But those who had spent six years of seminary training in Rome were divided too. Most loved Rome – and Alfred could see that John Salvatori was one of these. A smaller group were less enthusiastic – and Alfred himself had become one of these.

John Salvatori had loved Rome. He had spent six years at the College of Propaganda Fidei on the Janiculum, which had given him a certain status which he would never have had if he had stayed in Trinidad. His Roman education had marked him out as a priest, and he had taken some care that it should do so. Not for him the ordinary grind; nothing had been too tedious for John Salvatori, if it meant a centimetre of progress up the ladder of patronage. He had taken the trouble to learn Italian as quickly as possible, which had given him a head start over the other foreigners. He had charmingly made himself indispensable to those who taught him, to lowly priests, to Monsignori, to Bishops, even to Cardinals, when they swam into his orbit. He had kissed the Papal hand with burning, even passionate, lips. There had been no limit to his keenness to serve.

Yet, as Alfred was quick to realise as he listened to Salvatori's Roman memories, all this effort had led to a success so partial it might even have been called failure by some. Salvatori had studied Canon Law in his final two years, in the hope that this would be his passport into the Accademia – but this had not happened. He alluded to this failure to be recruited by the Accademia with a wistfulness that seemed more assumed than real. It was almost impossible to be wistful about the Accademia: it was the pinnacle of the Roman world, the training school for future bishops, the place where the Vatican diplomats were formed. Alfred himself had spent several years there before and after his ordination as a Bishop. Its doors had not been closed to him.

As they sat at supper – any idea of reading had been abandoned by Alfred, so interested was he in the conversation – the topic of the Accademia hung between them. Alfred knew he was a Palmer-Ross, he was someone. ('Are they anyone?' he could remember his mother asking about 'new' people.) The Pontifical

Academy for Noble Ecclesiastics, to use its full title, had accepted him. Alfred had been born into that world, but John Salvatori had not. Salvatori's mother's family, Alfred knew, were something to do with oil – just like the Barratts. His father had been an Italian about whom nothing certain was known. By contrast, everyone in Trinidad knew about the Palmer-Rosses. People – at least the type of people who went to the races on the Savannah and had drinks in the Queen's Park Hotel – simply knew. Alfred himself knew who was related to whom – he had even recognised a limited form of kinship with Mr Barratt – though his information was about a generation out of date, thanks to twenty years of isolation. But even so, he knew about Trinidad Society, and saw that John Salvatori was a man who had made his way in it almost entirely by his own efforts. He wondered why he did not resent this. He was amazed at the sheer amount of effort the man must have expended in order to have the dubious privilege of having tea or rum-and-Coke with a few heavily-accented old ladies.

Alfred himself was in the unusual position of having retired from the field. Once he had loved Rome, but now the memory of it rather embarrassed him. He was ashamed of his younger self, and the thought of how he had valued so many worthless things now made him feel uncomfortable. From this discomfort, John Salvatori was providing much relief. It was refreshing to see the man's innocence. Salvatori could actually do things – he could plan a new Cathedral, he could organise the collection of money. He could think, and think ahead too. Alfred's mind, by contrast, was paralysed by twenty years of inactivity. Something stopped him from doing anything: perhaps it was guilt, or some creeping realisation of the futility of all human action which sprang from that act, twenty-seven years ago, that had led to the conception of Simon Palmer. Fortunately, Salvatori's presence and conversation helped dispel the gloomiest of these thoughts, and he was able to go to bed almost amused by the distant prospect of a new Cathedral.

7

MR BARRATT lived in a concrete bungalow, quite close to the ill-fated Paradise Pastures where his wife had befriended the doctor. His house was huddled against the hillside with other concrete bungalows of identical design, as if it were seeking safety in numbers.

That morning it was silence that awoke him. His first thought was that this was the day on which he was to deliver the ultimatum to his clerks; his second thought was that it was so quiet. As a child in Port of Spain he had had a bedroom next to his father's, and the sound of snoring had kept him awake; but the sound had also comforted him as he lay awake in the dark – for as long as you could hear the old man snore you could be sure that he was alive and well. The slightest pause in the snoring was always worrying. And now, the same dead silence oppressed him, the silence that he had always feared as a boy. Someone was dead. It was the dog. The animal had stopped barking. A great sense of relief flooded over Mr Barratt. His neighbour's dog had been the bane of his life. He had to make sure that the animal was really dead. He got up to see with something that almost resembled energy.

It was in fact so.

In the small dust bowl, sometimes called a garden, but more often the yard, which divided his house from that of the Chief of Police, Mr Barratt saw the prone figure of what had been the Alsatian. Next to it stood the Chief, leaning on a spade, motionless.

'What has happened, Chief?' asked Barratt, from his doorstep.

'Someone took a dislike to my poor dog,' replied the Chief.

Mr Barratt felt a stab of guilt. Here he was rejoicing in what was clearly something of a domestic tragedy. And if someone had murdered the dog, then surely he had to be the chief suspect. He had certainly wanted to do so often enough.

'She's been in this yard for six years,' the Chief was saying, 'and now someone has poisoned her.'

Mr Barratt advanced on bare feet to take a closer look at the victim of this crime; he did so gingerly, for his feet were tender and the ground was stony; but he felt he had to pay his last respects, for the Chief was a nice enough man, and his next-door neighbour. It paid not to antagonise one's next-door neighbour. The unfortunate dog lay at the furthest extent of its chain, curled up, with one of its feet sticking awkwardly into the air. Clearly it had expired in some discomfort; Mr Barratt began to feel sorry for the dog too, as well as for its bereaved owner.

'Are you sure she has been poisoned?' he asked, not daring to refer to the Alsatian as 'it'.

'It is the way she is lying,' explained the Chief of Police. 'It shows that she has been poisoned.'

This was not a very scientific deduction, thought Mr Barratt; but as the Chief already had tears in his eyes, this was clearly not the time for an argument. The dog was certainly dead and that surely was enough. From now on he would be able to sleep without being woken up in the morning or in the middle of the night by its demented barking. He only hoped that the Chief would not rush out and get another dog too soon.

There was thus a lightness in his step as he walked to Da Silva that morning. He felt almost jaunty, something he had not felt for years. Perhaps this was why he tackled the question of the office spy with a degree of ferocity that was quite alien to him. His underlings were not accustomed to seeing him at such an early hour in their part of the building: indeed, they had rather got used to not seeing him at all of late. His sudden appearance in their midst produced looks of dismay on their normally guarded faces, and it was this dismay that Mr Barratt – and

Simon from his high desk – saw and interpreted as collective guilt. It was almost as good as a confession; to think that these criminals had been making a fool of him for years; it was too much, and the thought of it produced a blinding rage and a torrent of words.

It is not necessary to give details of Mr Barratt's speech, for it was hardly concise or coherent, being the fruit of years of repressed resentment. The six clerks before him, had they but realised it, bore the brunt of all the inefficiency, all the waste, all the stupidity that Barratt had ever endured in Trinidad. They were subjected to a condemnation of their entire way of life; they were told that they were a lazy bunch of good-for-nothing layabouts and that they could go and work for Mr Seth if they so desired. The peroration intimated that they were sacked and had a few moments to leave the building. In his anger Mr Barratt made the fateful utterance 'You are all the same.' Then he left to withdraw, so he thought, in triumph from the field.

It was a triumph of sorts. In menacing silence the six clerks tidied their desks and prepared to leave the building. They did so with the type of slowness that one could only assume was meant to convey to Simon that they wanted him to know that they were not intimidated. Simon watched them go; not one of them caught his eye. He realised that they thought he was the enemy. Mr Barratt's careless statement 'You are all the same' came back to him; he felt acutely uncomfortable about it. Perhaps there was something in this blanket condemnation after all. He was all too aware that he had to go and call on Mr Seth that very afternoon – not because he wanted to, but because Father Salvatori had more or less forced him into it. Yet Mr Barratt had just denounced and sacked all his employees bar one for this very crime – associating with Mr Seth. How on earth was he going to ask Mr Barratt's permission to leave the office for an hour or two in order to visit Mr Seth? It was not as if his visit to Seth could possibly be beneficial to Da Silva – he did not have the necessary dishonesty to use that as an excuse. It was all becoming far too complicated. He decided that the only thing to do was to try and use the least deception possible. He would leave the office without saying where he was going, as if he were going out for a late lunch. In all likelihood Mr Barratt would not even notice his absence.

*

He escaped at twenty past one; and Father Salvatori was in the Bishop's front garden, waiting for him as he came up the hill.

'I have to be back at the office quite soon,' he said, already making his excuses in advance. 'I don't think I'll be able to stay for long.'

'You can always leave me there once I've got into the presence,' said the priest cheerfully.

They walked on in silence until they were alongside the blank featureless wall. When they reached the metal gates, which in the sun seemed almost burning to the touch, Simon rang the bell and presented his face for inspection to the camera. The metal doors sprang open. In the cool shadows behind stood Burke. He looked at the priest with momentary suspicion but, perhaps remembering that he had orders to admit Simon whenever he called, he motioned them both to follow him. They followed him down the shadowy concrete path, which, so often had he cast his mind over that first visit, was now as familiar to Simon as any landscape in a recurring nightmare. But Father Salvatori, in his innocence, seemed to see nothing amiss in the shady garden or the maids who sat in the kitchen, still as death behind the louvred windows; nor did he seem to find it unusual that the interior of the house was in shuttered darkness; he seemed to be oblivious to the oddness that Simon felt about the place, so keen was he to seek out what was lost.

'I expected you,' said Mr Seth once they were in front of his desk in the air-conditioned study. He said this looking at Simon, as if there were no one else there.

'This is the Vicar-General of the diocese,' said Simon uncomfortably.

Father Salvatori smiled his very best smile at the one-eyed man.

'I am delighted to see him,'said Seth. 'The clergy very rarely come to visit me. Burke, perhaps you would be so kind as to give the Vicar-General a guided tour of the grounds and bring him back here in about ten minutes' time ...'

Simon found himself alone with Mr Seth.

'It seems that our friend Mr Barratt has been rather rash,' said Seth. 'To sack those six boys all at once, especially when they had done nothing to deserve it, seems almost colonial in its arrogance. They came up here and told me all about it. They think that I can do something for them. People often have this idea about me, that I am able to get things done for them. I try never to turn anyone away. In this case I was able to tell them that I thought all would be well, because Mr Barratt would be sure to change his mind.'

'Why would he do that?'

'He will change his mind,' said Mr Seth simply, ' – he will change his mind because you will persuade him to do so.'

Simon decided not to answer. Presently Mr Seth began to speak again, using those arts of persuasion with which he was most familiar.

'I fear that Mr Barratt is not a man who thinks in a reasonable way at all. He might be most unreasonable with you if he were to know that you were here. He is not a man to be trusted; he thinks that you are all the same. I know that the six boys are all lazy and stupid, though I am sure that you are not, but little good it does you when your employer thinks that you are all the same. The white man never has been fair to us and never will be. No matter how hard we work for him, ours is the effort and his is the praise.'

'I still don't understand quite what it is that you want me to do,' said Simon, interrupting the old man's flow, before he found its force too much for him. For Mr Seth was very persuasive indeed, and like that famous snake in the garden of Eden he knew his victim's weak points.

'I would like to see you as manager of Da Silva,' said Seth. 'Mr

Barratt has shown he isn't the man. If you were there, it would be such a wonderful opportunity.'

'For whom?'

'For all of us,' said Mr Seth. 'But especially for you and for me.'

'But Mr Barratt is not going to resign.'

'But perhaps he should.'

'That doesn't mean that he will,' said Simon.

'It is not something that you need to understand in any detail,' said Mr Seth. 'And now I really must devote some time to my other visitor. I told you I try never to turn anyone away. You must stay to lunch here. Burke will see to it that you are well fed. Here he is.'

There was a knock on the door, announcing the return of Father Salvatori and Burke.

'I have to get back to the office,' said Simon.

'But I will not allow you to,' said Seth with a smile. 'You are my guest. Burke will see to it.'

There was no arguing with such insistence, and Simon was handed over to the custody of Burke, who took him to the table by the pool-side. A bottle of whisky stood on the table. Burke withdrew, and Simon was left in solitary confinement. He poured himself some whisky and wondered if he was being watched. He suspected he was. Perhaps he simply ought to get up and walk away. How would they be able to stop him? Perhaps it wasn't too late even now just to walk away from the whole thing and leave Father Salvatori there. He should never have come. But immediately he remembered what Seth had said, and he knew that there was truth in it. That was what was so devilish about the man. Barratt was incompetent, and Simon knew that he himself could do his job so much better. And Barratt has said in his anger that they were all the same. Was he one of them after all? Seth thought so; the clerks thought so; and he himself began to think that he really owed Mr Barratt no gratitude at all.

Perhaps he ought not to drink whisky. He very rarely did. It seemed to heighten his passions. It was making him angry. Presently the first course arrived, brought by the girl he had seen on his first visit, the girl in the bikini. The first course consisted of a plate of defrosting prawns which she put down in front of him, before hurrying away.

There was to be no conversation to relieve his mind. It was getting late; even if he were to set off for the office at once, it was probably already too late. Perhaps he had better not go back to the office at all, but tell Mr Barratt that he had gone home because he was feeling ill, when he asked him tomorrow where he had been. He cursed the fate that condemned him to lie. But that was the trouble: you started with a small lie and eventually you had to tell bigger ones to cover them up.

The girl was coming back. Perhaps it was the effect of the whisky, but she was, he now realised – and not for the first time – just the sort of girl that he liked. She was about his own age, with smooth dark skin and pretty features, which, he imagined, would be soft to the touch. He wondered who she was, and what she was doing living in this strange enclosed world. He was sure he had never seen her in San Fernando. Presumably she spent all her time up in the house, shut away behind the metal gates and the high blank wall. Perhaps she was married to Burke, or even a relation of Seth's; but that did not seem very likely. He could not imagine Seth having any relations, or Burke having a wife. They were both too strange for the normality of families or marriage – for, never having experienced either, Simon tended to idealise the ordinariness of marriage and the family. Perhaps she was a daughter of one of the silent maids in the kitchen.

'Who are you?' he asked her as she leaned over to take his plate.

She smiled but did not answer. Then she went away and came back with another plate. It bore a steak. Simon had never had so much luxurious food before.

'Won't you sit down?' he asked her.

Silently, she drew up a chair.

He wondered if she were a mute. You did hear about mute women, who had had their tongues surgically removed so that they might never tell what they had seen. No one in this house

70

seemed to talk; he had heard Burke talk – but only a few words. The maids seemed to live in silence. Seth spoke, but in a tremulous and low voice, not in the open air but in a cold dark room; he lived among silences. Perhaps this girl was under some dreadful compulsion, kept here against her will. But she seemed happy enough. Then it occurred to him that perhaps she took her orders from Seth and had been sent to entertain him; perhaps she too was a temptation.

'Where is Father Salvatori?' he asked, sensing the danger of being alone with her.

'No one will disturb us here,' she said. 'Burke is busy with the boss.'

She did speak after all.

Simon looked at the pool and its icy blue water. Then he looked at his half-eaten steak, and then at his wrist-watch. The time for leaving was gone. And now he suddenly felt that it was too late, and that he had better stay after all. The girl, by breaking the silence, had achieved her purpose. He thought of the dank and cheerless flat where he lived alone in the town and of the lonely evenings he passed there. Ever since his mother had died he had tried to comfort himself with thoughts of future prosperity and marriage. He had been taught the value of saving up and hard work by his mother's example. But how pointless all that self-sacrifice now seemed. There was – though as a Catholic he did not realise it – a Puritan streak in his character. He did not drink whisky or smoke – except when he came to Mr Seth's. He had worked hard and saved and was loyal to his employer – until he met Mr Seth. He had never chased girls. His mother had left him a shining example of how even a momentary lapse in morality could lead to a lifetime of regret. And yet despite all this, despite all the reasons, like his mother before him, and perhaps like his unknown father, he now felt the passion that had led to his creation overtaking him, conquering twenty-seven years of caution.

He was falling in love.

Without touching, and without moving, they looked at each

71

other over the table, and their eyes met in a visual embrace. He felt at that moment that he knew her and that he wanted to be known by her just as deeply in return.

Father Salvatori appeared, accompanied by Burke, and the interesting moment was gone. The girl got up and went into the house very quickly, as if she were afraid of Burke, and he was left alone, as if he had never had a companion.

'I've had a long talk with our friend,' said Salvatori, taking the girl's place, hardly aware that she had been there, and holding out a glass, which Burke filled with whisky and water.

'It has been a most enlightening talk,' he added.

'Oh?' said Simon stupidly.

'Aren't you going to ask me what it was about?' asked Salvatori archly. 'Naturally we talked about you and the new Cathedral. Mr Seth has given me a cheque. He really has been most generous. Look.'

Simon took the cheque. It was for fifty-thousand dollars.

'Not US dollars, I know,' said the priest, thinking he was reading his mind. 'But it is a good start and there will be much more to come. He promised that. And he tells me that he is a man who keeps his promises. He also knows the people who can actually do the work for us; he has influence in the construction trade. You could look a little bit more enthusiastic. He has taken an enormous liking to you. He told me that the only thing wrong with you was that you lack ambition. And I think I know the reason why.'

'Why?'

'Mr Seth says that you are content to be second-in-command at Da Silva, even though you are the ideal man to run the place. You see, you don't have enough faith in your own abilities. And it is all because of your parentage.'

'The only person who knows about that is my mother and she is dead,' said Simon shortly.

'I know,' said Salvatori. 'I used to know her by sight. And that is how and why I know that you are of mixed race. Never mind who your father was, but he wasn't a dark man. An awful lot of people in Trinidad are of mixed race – even the Archbishop – but it doesn't mean that you have to take second place. You must let Mr Seth help you.'

'And what will he get out of it?'

'A useful contact. Those sorts of things are important for men of business. It all works by word of mouth. You know that. Of course he stands to gain, but so do you. It is the same with the Cathedral.' His voice warmed, for the Cathedral was now nearly a reality. 'He wants to help build the Cathedral, because that is a thing people like doing. He will have the added reputation of a church-builder, and we will have a new church. That way everyone benefits.'

'I think I should go home,' said Simon. 'Perhaps the sun has made my head ache, or perhaps it is the whisky.'

'But see Mr Seth before you go,' urged the priest.

'I'd much rather just go.'

'No, please see him,' insisted Salvatori. 'He asked me to make sure you saw him before you went. And he has been so kind over the Cathedral ...'

This note of insistence in his voice betrayed the fact that a bargain had been made, and that Father Salvatori was keen to fulfil his side of it. Simon realised that his case was hopeless. He had to see Seth and he would have to give in to him. The Cathedral depended on it; his future employment depended on it, for if Mr Barratt were to know where he had spent the afternoon, he would surely be sacked. And finally, he knew he wanted to see the girl again. Besides, he was used to trusting the clergy.

'Oh, very well then,' he said.

8

THE BISHOP had passed his day in his usual solitariness, but towards sundown he had begun to sense once again that isolation was losing its charms. This realisation had been sparked by the remembrance of how keen Father Salvatori had been to leave the lunch table that day. Alfred had noticed his impatience; evidently the young man had had business that needed seeing to. Naturally, he had not asked what that business might be. He would not have dreamed of showing such a vulgar curiosity; but like a lot of people who do not want to be seen to be vulgarly curious, he was in fact so. What did Father Salvatori – or anyone else for that matter – find to do? After all, people like Father Salvatori had to make their own work; they did not have to be office slaves, but they seemed to be as busy as anyone who worked set hours. Where did all this activity come from? How did they find so many things to fill their days? Alfred was careful to distinguish between activity and occupation. He himself was always occupied. He said Mass, he prayed in his private chapel, he read the newspapers, he had meals, he studied sections of the *Summa Theologica*, he dealt with various pieces of correspondence. In the evening he liked to read improving novels by George Eliot or Sir Walter Scott. Thus was he occupied. Activity, however, was something else entirely. Activity was what went on in the town of San Fernando. Activity had even invaded the Church. Naturally, Alfred had nothing against the Second Vatican Council; but he had deep reservations about something called 'the spirit of Vatican Two'. It was this spirit that had incited people to frenetic activity where before there had been the calm of centuries. Father Salvatori was clearly in this mould. He would knock down the Cathedral and replace it with a durable piece of concrete. He would galvanise and organise the laity. He would even, given time, have a steel band playing at Mass. He was clearly a man of activity.

The odd thing was that much as he felt he ought to disapprove, Alfred found that he liked John Salvatori and his spirit of activity. He was rather taken by the contrast between Salvatori and himself. One did hear of opposites attracting each other. In fact it was a strong liking that he could feel developing. This had troubled him for most of the afternoon. After he had seen Salvatori rush off after lunch, he had been forced to reflect on all the places he had ever lived in, places where the hours after luncheon had been devoted to idleness. In Rome, people had gone to bed after lunch and stayed there until five. No one had ever rushed off to do anything in the searing heat of the day. Trinidad was no different. The most useful part of the day was usually over by noon. No one rushed to do things after lunch in Trinidad, as far as Alfred knew. It made him envious – an odd sensation which he had not at first recognised – to think that John Salvatori had so many things to do.

The fact that he liked the man was troublesome to his conscience. He had analysed the feeling for several hours. There were several good reasons for liking John Salvatori. Archbishop Nourganian had plainly been most fond of him, which gave any liking Alfred might have the force of precedent. He was of pleasant appearance and was keen to please without being unctuous. In addition to this, he was the ideal companion for a Bishop, being a priest and yet on a lower rung of the clerical ladder. As Vicar-General, John Salvatori seemed delicately aware of his inferior position; he was full of respect; he knew his place; and such knowledge was a necessary part of being a social climber.

It was this that worried Alfred. John Salvatori was clearly a climber, even a social climber. He could hardly be anything else. The Church despite, or perhaps because of, the spirit of Vatican Two was the last refuge on earth for social climbers. Only in the Church could a peasant end up as a Pope, as had happened with John XXIII. On a lesser scale, someone like Salvatori could enter the Church and end up on intimate terms with Alfred Palmer-Ross, who, if Salvatori had never been ordained, would never in the normal course of things have met him. In that sense too, the Church was a great leveller. It gave opportunities to all. Yet, thought Alfred to himself, birth should have its claim. This sounded like an absurd eighteenth-century view, he knew, except for one thing. Simon Palmer had a claim on him by his birth. It was this that troubled his conscience. He really had no business liking Father Salvatori: any such affection should be directed towards Simon Palmer. He owed so much to Simon, for he had neglected him so long; and if he were to befriend anyone it should be Simon and not John Salvatori.

The ideal solution, to treat both with complete impartiality, was fast becoming beyond him. He had been dispassionate for far too long already. The careful balance of his emotions had now been disturbed. That very afternoon he had been wondering what John Salvatori was doing: this was in itself quite absurd when one remembered that he had hardly given a thought to another human being in the last twenty years. That was why he felt guilty about Simon Palmer.

Simon Palmer was so deserving; and he deserved well in particular from the father who had ignored his existence ever since his birth. There were various excuses that Alfred had for this omission. His mother had never asked for anything; it had never crossed his mind that she might have had anything to ask for. He had not thought about her or the boy because he had wanted to block the whole episode out of his consciousness. He was frightened that if he had thought about them he would have ended up hating them. After all, it was the existence of the woman and her child that was responsible for his exile in San Fernando. He had been afraid of blaming them. And so it had turned out that Simon, who bore half his surname, was a second-rate clerk with Da Silva. He could have sent him to University, perhaps to England, where he would have escaped the narrow confines of Trinidadian life. But all that was now too late; the boy had grown up not knowing anything other than Trinidad. He was his mother's son, not his father's. He was the son of a woman who had kept a fent-shop in Port of Spain, not the son of a Palmer-Ross. Perhaps this was his mother's revenge; perhaps she had wanted to bring him up in such a way so that Alfred could have no part in him. If so, she had succeeded. However, there still remained the tie of blood. Perhaps he ought to make a new will in Simon Palmer's favour. That had drawbacks: Alfred thought that he might easily live another twenty years, and what good would all the money be to Simon in twenty years' time? If he needed money he needed it now.

Father Salvatori came back. Alfred heard the front door open and stood still. He had left the door of the drawing-room open, deliberately and invitingly so. As he had hoped, he heard the clerical footsteps pause in the hallway, and then a cautious head poked round the door.

'Do come in,' Alfred managed to say with a greater degree of warmth in his voice than he had used in years. 'You must tell me more about your new Cathedral.'

'It is already taking shape, my lord,' said Salvatori. 'You might like to look at this.'

He took out his wallet and carefully extracted Seth's cheque. He handed it to Alfred.

'Fifty-thousand dollars,' said Alfred. 'I suppose that means that work can start almost immediately.'

'It can indeed. And when work starts it has a way of gathering momentum. Funds start to pour in when people actually see that something is being built.'

'And who is this generous Mr Seth?' asked Alfred, studying the cheque, before giving it back. 'Do I know him?'

'Yes, he is very generous,' said Salvatori. 'And he told me that this contribution is only a start. Concrete is the cheapest building material, and we seem to be half way there already, as Mr Seth actually has the men to build the place for us. He spoke of forming his own construction company just for this job. The whole thing shouldn't take long. As for your knowing him – I very much doubt it.'

'Isn't he a Catholic?'

'No, he isn't, but he does seem to have a certain amount of natural piety. He seems to think that the building of a proper church here is a good thing. He has got a lot of money and he told me that he would like to spend some on good works before he died, rather than after. He was born here, and thus the Cathedral of his home town seemed the natural choice.'

'I see. If he is the richest man here, then he is a sort of local patron, isn't he?' said Alfred, noting that Salvatori seemed very impressed by money, whoever its owner was.

'He is certainly rich,' said Salvatori, remembering all he had seen. 'He owns the house at the top of the hill.'

'I have noticed his garden wall. I suppose he is a black man?'

'Yes.'

'I suppose too he wants to show off his wealth – or am I being unjust?'

'He lives a very discreet life,' said Salvatori carefully. 'You would never really know what was behind that high wall unless someone told you. He has a huge house and garden, with a swimming-pool, but there is no deliberate ostentation. He seems to like a quiet life as far as I can see; he never goes out and flaunts his riches – but that is probably the result of an unfortunate deformity.'

'Oh yes?' asked Alfred.

'It really does make him hideous to look at,' said Salvatori with an elegant little shudder. 'One of his eyes has been gouged out – not surgically removed, but torn out – and the empty socket is surrounded by scars. It looks as though he's been ravaged by a shark.'

'Couldn't he wear an eye-patch?' asked Alfred. 'I mean, if one is deformed it seems best to hide it from the world ...'

'I suppose he could, but chooses not to. It is almost as if his deformity is some sort of challenge. I think he expects you to look at him in all his ugliness. It is an odd sort of honesty.'

'Well, I do admire your bravery in going up there and facing him. It shows that you are truly devoted to the new Cathedral. And how did this charming Mr Seth make all his money?'

'Oh,' said Salvatori, suddenly vague. 'He used to work in Port of Spain, and now he has various property interests.'

'I've heard that too,' said Alfred. 'The manager of Da Silva says that Seth owns their building and is trying to evict them when their lease is up.'

'They seem to be negotiating over something,' said Salvatori, wondering how much the Bishop really knew. 'Simon Palmer was up there this afternoon, and he seems to get on with Mr Seth very well, as far as I could see.'

'John,' said the Bishop all of a sudden, 'if you go into the dining-room, you will find a bottle of rum and some glasses in the sideboard.'

Salvatori got up. Alfred heard him clanking around in the dining-room and tried to compose his thoughts. The Vicar-General reappeared with bottle, tray and glasses.

'Say when,' he said as he poured Alfred a drink. Alfred held out his glass, thinking that the phrase was rather arch, what his mother would have called 'common'.

'I know this Simon Palmer,' said Alfred casually. 'I think I have met him on two occasions, or perhaps three. He has been in San Fernando a month or so, and Archbishop Nourganian sent him here with a letter of introduction.'

'Did he?' said Salvatori, settling down with a drink and sensing gossip in the air. 'May I smoke? Thank you. Of course, the Archbishop was always very fond of him, you know. Simon Palmer was a bit of a hobby with him, and that was how I got to know him too. Whenever I had to be at Archbishop's House' – Alfred imagined that John Salvatori had had frequent cause to be there, right at the centre of things – 'I'd either hear about him or see him. There were all sorts of rumours about Palmer, you know. People would even say that he was Archbishop Nour-ganian's son.'

'But that is ridiculous,' said Alfred immediately. 'The boy

79

couldn't possibly be related to him, as he is black, and Nour-ganian is an Armenian.'

Salvatori was a little taken aback by the insistence of the Bishop's tone. This was not the usual detachment that one expected from Alfred Palmer-Ross.

'I am only repeating what people said,' he remarked defen-sively. 'Naturally I never believed it for a moment. But people always will make what they can out of what they take to be evidence: and it certainly was true that the Archbishop was fond of Simon Palmer. Someone paid the boy's school fees at the college in Port of Spain, and it certainly wasn't the boy's mother, who kept a shop that sold God knows what. It was generally assumed that the Archbishop paid the fees. And as for the racial question, I would hardly describe Simon Palmer as black, because he is clearly more white than black, and certainly whiter than his mother. An Armenian father is a possibility at least.'

'Yes, of course,' conceded Alfred. 'The Armenians are a Cau-casian race. But I find the whole thing most unlikely. If the Archbishop has been kind to the boy, all that proves is what we've always known, namely that Alphonsus is a very kind man.'

'That is exactly my opinion,' said Salvatori, lighting a ciga-rette. 'The Archbishop was kind to a boy who, if the truth were known, had a far from easy childhood.'

'And what is the truth?' asked Alfred.

'The truth is,' said John Salvatori, with all the relish that discussing the misfortunes of others brings, 'the truth is that young Simon was the product of a supposed maternal indiscre-tion. She came to Port of Spain years ago from Tobago, and never once mentioned the boy's father, either to him or anyone else. The fact that it was all a big secret led to all the speculation. People would assume it was the Archbishop, because they as-sumed the father was someone important, someone who could afford to pay the fees. But in fact, as I have said, no one knows for certain, the mother told no one, and she's now dead. You see, she couldn't tell anyone, because the whole thing was so dis-graceful. I know,' he continued, anticipating an objection, 'that thirty per cent of the population is illegitimate, and as it's so common it is hardly a disgrace, even, God knows, among the Catholics. Then why was she so tight-lipped about the whole thing? The only logical explanation is that it wasn't her indiscretion at all. She had been raped by some white man, and she was keeping quiet about it in case anyone tried to avenge the wrong. You see, the boy himself might even have tried to avenge her when he grew up. People here are very hot on revenge.'

'Goodness, you do have an imagination,' said Alfred. 'Do you think that is what the boy himself thinks?'

'I doubt if he thinks much about it at all,' said Salvatori, allowing his glass to be refilled. 'I have spoken to him and I think he is remarkably content with little, and not at all ambitious except for ordinary things. Now, if he were to throw in his lot with Mr Seth he could do very well for himself.'

'Has Mr Seth made him some sort of an offer?'

'Yes. He told me so himself. Mr Seth wants to get rid of Mr Barratt and have Palmer run Da Silva.'

'This Mr Seth seems to be everywhere,' mused Alfred. 'It is strange to think that I have lived here so long and only just become aware of his identity. Until now he has been an invisible presence. He will build our new Cathedral. But tell me, John' – he had slipped without noticing it into calling the young man by his Christian name – 'is it possible that we may regret putting ourselves so much in Mr Seth's debt?'

'I don't see how we can,' said Salvatori. 'It is not as though we are in a position to do him any favours, is it? He has nothing to gain from us. And besides, he seems to have everything already.'

'Is he respectable?' asked Alfred. 'Or is he going to build the Cathedral to buy respectability?'

'That is common enough; but as long as the end product is good, we have no right to complain if the motive is tainted.'

'Well, I am glad that you are satisfied,' said Alfred, and resolved to say no more on the matter.

The conversation, however, had been most enlightening. Alfred realised that John Salvatori was not very careful about his associates. He saw money as money and was not bothered about where it came from. There was something rather coarse in this. He wondered whether Seth and Salvatori were not in fact very well matched; by this he did not mean that Salvatori was a criminal (for he had little clear picture about Seth as yet), but rather an irreligious materialist who built Cathedrals, not for the greater Glory of God, but for the greater glory of himself.

*

Darkness had fallen over San Fernando. Simon sat in his flat meditating on the events of the day. The flat was small and comfortless; his landlady lived below and had furnished the place in the true West Indian vernacular. There was furniture covered with plastic. There was a formica-topped table. There were louvred glass windows. There was none of the bare wooden elegance of the Bishop's house, nor even the concrete chic of Mr Barratt's undeniably ill-kept bungalow.

He had got back to Da Silva at about four that afternoon, and as yet he had no idea whether Mr Barratt knew of his absence or where he had been. But if it were to emerge that he had been at Seth's, it would make him a fellow conspirator with the sacked clerks, whose absence haunted the empty office.

Simon had always prided himself on his honesty, and rightly so, for he knew that it was a rare virtue. When he was twenty-one, like most other people he had voted in the elections for the Professor and his party – but at that time no one knew about the Professor's real character, or so they had assured themselves. No one ever knew until it was too late; one always fooled oneself, if that was what one needed to do. But deep down one knew, and could not escape the fact that corruption and theft were in the nation's bloodstream. Simon certainly knew it, and such knowledge meant that he was in some way not as innocent as he would have liked to have been. He had tried not to be compromised. In Port of Spain he had kept the books scrupulously and never skimmed off a single dollar for himself. This reputation for honesty had won him promotion to being second-in-command in San Fernando. And now his reputation was about to be ruined – in fact, was as good as ruined – by an association with Mr Seth which he had not sought or wanted. Even if he were to explain the circumstances, though, who would believe him? Who would believe that he had gone to see an arch-criminal at the behest of his boss, or because Father Salvatori was seeking an introduction? No one would ever believe that. Far more credible was the idea that he had gone there seeking his own advantage. Dishonesty and self-seeking were the common way of life, after all.

Ironically, there was something about financial corruption and its rewards that repelled him. If Seth were to use Da Silva as a front for whatever project he had in mind, then certainly Simon would profit by it. But the thought of large amounts of money for little or no effort did not attract him. There had to be something more to life than sitting around in idleness and getting paid large sums for it. That appealed to a lot of people but not to him. Perhaps his mother had brought him up too strictly, or the Archbishop had given him too good an example, but there it was: if he was to be rich, he wanted the satisfaction of knowing he deserved to be rich.

The awfulness of his position consisted in this: he was about to be given what so many sought against his will. It all depended on what Mr Seth would do next. He was in his power. He had swum into his orbit and had not the means to tear himself free. If it had been purely a matter of money, perhaps he might have broken free by an act of the will; but there was something he could not resist, and that was the girl who lived in Seth's house.

He still had no clear idea who she was. She was young and she was beautiful and he wanted her – all that was clear enough. But who she was was quite obscure. He could not imagine what she did in that strange household. Surely she could not hang around the pool-side all day. Presumably she had other clothes apart from her bikini. She had appeared to him like a vision, a phantom, someone who did not seem to have any ties with the rest of the world. Real people, Simon knew, were not like that. Where one person stopped, another began. Other people defined you: but she seemed to exist isolated in space and time. Because his imagination was freed from the usual banal restraints that ordinary life imposed, he could think what he liked about her. Anything was possible. This was surely Seth's most devilish temptation yet. Perhaps money could not move him, but the old man had guessed that something else might work where filthy lucre had failed. Simon knew that the old man had judged his victim rightly, and that he had found the chink in his armour. It frightened him to think that Mr Seth could see into his soul. Or perhaps it was simply the case that the old man had a shrewd general idea about human nature and knew that every 27-year-old would desire a pretty girl.

He was now sure that Mr Seth was somehow offering her to him. She was the bait. They had been left alone together the second time he had called there. Mr Seth recognised that she was useful and had thrown her in his way. But there was more to it than that: the girl wanted to be thrown in his way. Seth could hardly force her to act in this way, unless he really did have some terrifying power over her. No, she wanted to be a party to it, and the look she had given him was a sure sign of that. This made the temptation all the more real. In fact the stage called temptation was already over: that look they had exchanged had fixed things. He had more or less admitted to himself that he would go back there, in order to see the girl. And he would go back there soon. It would, he was equally sure, be a disaster in the long run; Mr Seth would ruin him, and no good could possibly come of their association. He was rushing towards what he ought to flee, but it was already too late to be reasonable or to try and do the right thing, when the desire to do the wrong one had already taken such strong hold of him. There was no going back. In his pocket he felt a card that Mr Seth had given him. On it was his private telephone number. He had been invited to ring whenever he wanted to. He thought of the girl and knew that he would. His pulse raced and the sound of his own blood pounded in his ears, the only sound that disturbed the still, tropical night.

*

The moon had risen over San Fernando. In another part of the town, Mr Barratt put out his light. He too had had a perplexing day, even a disturbing day. His decisive action that morning had as yet brought no tangible result. He had stormed at the clerks and told them they were sacked, but their reaction had unnerved him. It is true that they had left the office but they had done so in a spirit of menacing silence, as if they had expected what they had heard, and that they now knew what to do. That silence disturbed him; it was like the silence before a hurricane. It was as if his bombshell had fallen into the sea and not even made the slightest splash, but sunk without trace leaving but this eerie silence. For the rest of the day he had let time drift past him, as he wondered whether he had not lost the initiative completely. Perhaps the boys would simply turn up to work the next day, as if nothing had happened. What would he do then? If the greatest weapon an employer had was to be rendered useless, what would there be left for him to do?

Mr Barratt's uneasy mind faded into unconsciousness. It was in truth somewhat easier for him to get to sleep, now that the Chief of Police's dog had died. The hoarse barking was gone forever. But as is often the case when a persistent noise ceases, its echo lives on after it. As he slept, Mr Barratt dreamed of barking, wild and demented barking which gradually grew in volume and pitch until it became a sound so sharp as to be almost inaudible to the human ear.

The bullets, of which there were seven, woke him instantly and violently from his barking dream. He was too young to have been in the war, but some old race-memory made him keep his head under fire. Ignoring the shattered glass, he rolled out of bed and onto the floor. He crawled under the bed. Presently the firing stopped and a deathly silence followed.

Something similar, he remembered, had happened to an uncle of his in Kenya. (The Barratts had been a large family, and many had made their fortunes, or at least tried to, in far-flung parts of

85

the Empire.) This East African uncle had been shot at as he lay in bed, some time during the Mau Mau disturbances. The terrorists had hoped to induce the unfortunate old man to run out of his bungalow in search of help. Then they would shoot him in the open. But Uncle Reggie had been too clever for them and hidden under his bed all night. His wife had shown less heroic caution. How on earth his aunt's lumbering figure, built more for comfort than for speed, had been mistaken for that of Reginald Barratt of the Colonial Police Force was an enduring mystery. But the memory of what had happened to his aunt was enough to keep Mr Barratt from moving, resolved to stay under the bed until morning came.

As it was, however, the safety of morning was anticipated by the reassuring sound of a police car, its siren audible a long way off, giving both Mr Barratt and his assailants ample warning that help was on its way.

*

The girl heard the sound of the sirens too. She had been watching television, unable to sleep, but when the real sound of the police car, shrill in the night air, had mingled with the artificial noises coming from the television set, she had switched it off and gone out into the garden.

The noise died in the distance and all was still, apart from the gentle lapping of the water in the swimming-pool. The house felt empty, and she stood there in the humid night air, overwhelmed by solitude, sensing the house's desolation. She felt very much alone; somewhere, she knew, the Boss was asleep: but she sensed the absence of Burke and Payne, and she was frightened.

Perhaps she ought to go to bed, but she hesitated there in the garden, standing still in the dark, wondering what to do. Then, after a few moments, she sought reassurance by going into the kitchen and switching on the lights, trying to banish what troubled her with the harsh glare of neon. The maids were now at home, and the kitchen was hers. The freezer hummed in its corner. Inside it, she knew, were the imported luxuries that they lived off – steaks from America, New Zealand lamb, pink prawns from foreign seas, all very expensive, all products of far-off places of which she knew next to nothing. The sheer expensiveness of it all comforted her. Burke and Payne would come back, she knew, for no one could abandon such frozen solid advantages. And, with this to calm her, she padded on bare feet towards her empty bedroom.

9

SIMON had gone to the office with his mind still full of the girl, and was only jolted out of it by the news that someone had tried to murder Mr Barratt in the night.

The news had spread quickly. All the clerks, who had reported for work as normal, had heard about it. They seemed to have gleaned all the details, almost before they had taken place. Mr Barratt himself was not at the office but detained at home by the police, dealing with questions, or so Simon imagined. And because there was nothing to be done in the office – for how could one do any work in the circumstances? The clerks seemed strangely excited beneath their inscrutable looks – Simon set off to Mr Barratt's house to see if he could be of any use there, and drawn as well by a macabre curiosity. There was nothing quite like an attempted murder to make its victim interesting, he supposed, except a successful one.

He walked through the town, and passed the Cathedral, so intent on his journey that he did not notice that work had already started on the building; but he continued on his way towards Paradise Pastures, his head full of amazement that someone – who but Mr Seth? – had actually taken the step of shooting up Mr Barratt's house. The said house lay on the better side of the town – not actually in Paradise Pastures itself, the nearest thing to a prestigious address San Fernando could boast of – but in that direction. Simon had never been to Mr Barratt's house before, but he did have a vague idea where it was; nor was it hard to find, as there was a large police-car parked outside it. Leaning against the vehicle, smoking and armed to the teeth, lounged a policeman. The louvred windows displayed their smashed glass, and for the first time it sank home to Simon that violence had been done, and that this was no longer a mere game of words. From the broken windows he could hear voices. Rather than stand eavesdropping in the yard under the suspicious eyes of the policeman, and wishing to associate himself with the victim rather than the criminal, he made to go in. The policeman did not try to stop him, but held the door open for him. No one else had come snooping round, as people were too wise for that, so the policeman reckoned that this young man must have a purpose.

Simon stepped into the sitting-room of the bungalow and into the middle of the conversation he had heard from outside. Mr Barratt saw him and gestured him to a seat; he was standing in the middle of the room, and in the other chair was the Chief of Police – a prosperous, fat man, now squeezed into his uniform and looking most uncomfortable. Simon felt that he had walked into some trial and was there to be a witness, to be called if necessary.

'I know you are upset,' the Chief was saying, in tones of abject apology, as if the whole thing had been his fault. 'It is very frightening when this sort of thing happens; but I do think the whole thing isn't as you imagine ...'

'I am not upset, as you put it. I am angry. Nor am I frightened. It is just that someone tried to murder me last night and you don't seem to be too bothered about it.'

The Chief shook his head sadly. 'Oh no, Mr Barratt. No one has tried to murder you. If they had wanted to kill you, what was to stop them? They could have come in here and shot you in the head. They didn't need a gun at all; they could have crept in here and slit your throat when you were asleep. But they didn't. They merely fired a few shots through your window.'

'Merely?' said Barratt. 'They would have come in and murdered me if you fools hadn't turned up and frightened them off with your sirens blaring.'

'You should be grateful that the sirens saved your life, then.'

'The sirens gave the murderers a chance to get away in time. If you had come quietly you might have caught the bastards.'

Simon could sense that a quarrel was developing.

'They had already gone,' said the Chief. 'And we always use our sirens. It is the rule. And you are getting worked up about nothing. I am the one who should be upset, not you. No one tried to kill you, they tried to kill me. Our houses are next door to each other and they are identical. The criminals confused the left with the right. And the proof of the matter is that they had gone to the trouble of killing my dog the day before.'

'You care more about that bloody dog than you do about me.'

The Chief ignored the remark, which happened to be true, and started to give his reasoned account of the previous night's events.

'Look,' he said, as if he were explaining something to a dim child. 'First of all they kill the dog. So the job became possible. Then the very next night they come with their guns to frighten me, but they get the wrong house, because they can't tell their right from their left in the dark. Criminals are stupid, you know. But they aren't that stupid; they wouldn't want to kill you or frighten you. I am the Chief of Police, and I was the one they wanted to intimidate. No one would want to intimidate you, now, would they?'

'I happen to know that there are at least six people who would,' said Mr Barratt seriously. 'Palmer here will tell you the same thing. Yesterday I sacked, or at least gave notice to, the six clerks at Da Silva ...'

'And they came and fired on your house in revenge? How do a bunch of boys get hold of bullets and guns?'

The Chief leant back in his chair, thinking that this settled the argument.

'I don't think for a moment that they did it themselves,' said Barratt angrily. 'I think they went up the hill and spoke to Mr Seth who sent down one of his henchmen.'

The Chief looked less comfortable. The rhythm of the conversation was broken, and a silence fell between them. Barratt realised that at last he had made an impact on the Chief, that he had shown that he was not to be fooled any more. The Chief certainly seemed perplexed and suddenly out of his depth, as if he now realised that the problem could not be contained any more. The same thought had occurred to Simon. If Barratt were to denounce Seth publicly there was no knowing what might come of it.

'I don't know who you mean,' said the Chief at last, hoping that ignorance might be the best policy, when honesty was clearly too dangerous.

'Oh, I think you do,' said Barratt. 'He lives at the top of the hill and he has two thugs in permanent attendance on him; Palmer will tell you that much. The man is a gangster.'

'That is an awfully serious accusation to make against a man you have never even seen. Mr Seth is a reputable businessman,' he said, forgetting that he had just denied all knowledge of the man. 'Just because he is black ...'

'But I have never seen him,' said Barratt. 'How do I know what he is? I would have supposed he was an Indian. But obviously you have seen him, Chief.'

'What is that supposed to mean?'

'Nothing at all. I am sure you are as against organised crime and intimidation as I am. No doubt you will show the depth of your opposition by going up to Seth and arresting him. The man has some or all of my clerks in his pay. And when I sacked them because of it, Seth tried to put me out of the way.'

'There isn't a shred of evidence for that,' said the Chief.

'Oh God,' said Barratt wearily.

'They killed the dog before the clerks were sacked – how do you explain that?'

'I don't. I don't need to. Seth wants me out of the way so he can have Da Silva, and that is more than enough evidence.'

'I think you have an inflated idea of your own importance, Mr Barratt,' said the Chief, standing up to go. 'Good morning.'

The Chief made what he hoped was a dignified exit; however, to Simon, it merely seemed to be a highly embarrassed one.

'You see,' said Mr Barratt, bitterly, as soon as he was gone. 'You just have to mention that name. Seth runs the entire town. I think he has the police in his pocket. You saw how the Chief wilted at the name of Seth. Of course, what he said was all nonsense, about them wanting to kill him. He is trying to find an excuse, to make it seem that nothing has happened: the truth is that they won't investigate anything that Seth might have a hand in. Seth can do whatever he likes around here. He is untouchable. I might as well give in.'

'What do you mean by give in?'

'I could go up there and tell the man that I've decided to resign and go away. God alone knows, I hate this place. Why I stay I can't imagine; but I suppose I don't want Seth to have the satisfaction of having driven me out. I could take early retirement, and then Seth could have his own man in my place. He owns the freehold, and the people in Port of Spain don't care about it enough to take an interest. Some bright young man just needs to say that he alone can get the lease renewed and he'll have the job and be in Seth's debt forever. Seth will have what he wants and everyone will be happy.'

'But what does Seth want?' asked Simon. 'What will he do with Da Silva?'

'Import-export and no questions asked,' said Barratt. 'A tidy little operation. Something nice and legal to cover up his other activities.'

Simon was silent; he knew he was the bright young man that Seth had in mind.

'Are all the clerks in the office this morning?' asked Barratt.

'Yes, just as usual.'

'I suppose they think that I wouldn't be foolish enough to insist that they were sacked after my warning last night. They are right too. I'm not sure if I want to force Seth to kill me. Perhaps the best idea would be to close Da Silva down altogether, to kill the goose before it lays a golden egg. That would be a pity for you, though.'

'Yes,' said Simon.

'You'd be left high and dry,' said Mr Barratt thoughtfully. 'A pity, as I always thought you would do so well with the firm.'

'You did?'

'Yes.'

Mr Barratt got up and began to fumble around in a sideboard for a bottle and a glass.

'I don't think I'll come in to work today,' he said. 'I've had a shock. I don't want to see our employees. I don't want to give them that satisfaction. You go in and do the best you can. You'll have to. From now on I am going to be on sick leave.'

*

Simon left to return to Da Silva. The six clerks were there in the main room, sitting idly over their ledgers, as if this were an ordinary day like any other. Simon went into his office and sat down; he watched them through the glass panel. He wondered if Mr Barratt would ever return. Common sense certainly dictated a retirement from the field. The next time, if it came, Burke would kill him. Simon was sure that it was Burke who had fired the shots the night before. Burke looked like a murderer. It all seemed perfectly clear. On the other side of the glass he sensed that the clerks knew that they had won. They were in the pay of Mr Seth; he had proved that he could and would look after them; they were safe.

Mr Seth, Simon decided, was everywhere. The telephone rang, and he picked up the receiver, knowing who it would be.

'I do hope,' he heard Seth say, 'that poor Mr Barratt will get over the shock he must be feeling.'

'Then you know about it?'

'It has been all over the town. Nothing happens here without everyone knowing about it. Do come up and see me this afternoon. I am not alone.'

Simon understood the reference to the girl. 'I will tell Mr Barratt that I am coming,' he said.

'That will be excellent,' said Seth.

The line, as they say, went dead. Simon phoned Barratt to tell him where he was going. He was resolved to do nothing in secret. Barratt, hearing where he was going, knew he had been defeated.

*

As the day drew on, Mr Barratt became more and more depressed. Whisky and suspicions clouded his mind. That Seth had invited Palmer to see him, seemed to be evidence that there was some sort of a deal to be made. Seth had already corrupted the clerks and would now try to do the same with Palmer. In the darkness of his present frame of mind, Barratt realised that Seth would succeed; Palmer would be corrupted. All his suppressed distrust and dislike of black Trinidadians was coming to the surface of his mind. Seth had the Chief of Police in his control – the Chief who was his next-door neighbour, and who he had always thought was honest, if not very bright. How mistaken that now seemed: if anything, the Chief was dishonest and clever enough to see the profit to be had in being friendly with Seth. And he feared that he had made a similar mistake with Palmer. He too would be won over. Palmer, he now saw, was one of 'them', not one of 'us'. In any conflict the blacks would line up against the whites, irrespective of where justice lay. Race came first; the Chief, and the sacked clerks, Seth and Palmer were bound to stick close to each other. Without knowing it, Barratt had stumbled upon exactly the same argument that Seth had used with Simon.

Who was there he could trust? There was only one person who was immune to all this corruption, and that was Alfred Palmer-Ross. Seth could not have bought the Bishop. The Bishop's father had been Chief of the Port of Spain Colonial Police. His grandfather had been Chief Justice. He himself was a Bishop, albeit a Catholic one. Ross was probably the least corruptible man in Trinidad. He would go and see him. He had to talk to someone; he had to denounce Seth to someone who would listen to him, who would take him seriously. Thus he resolved to smarten up his appearance and go up to the place where the man lived, half way up the hill.

94

*

Father Salvatori was out, fortunately, having gone to visit an out-
lying parish, as Vicars-General were supposed to do, and thus unable
to intercept Mr Barratt in his errand. If he had been there, he most
certainly would have tried to do so. But, as it was, the housekeeper
let him in and thought he was sufficiently august a personage to be
allowed to see the Bishop. She rang the bell and left him in the
hallway. Alfred emerged from his study to be confronted by Barratt,
a large presence in the narrow space, still breathless from his climb
up from the town. There was no getting rid of such a man, thought
Alfred, with a sense that he was somehow being hounded by social
visits from people he did not want to see.

'How kind of you to return my visit,' he said with the hypocrisy
which is necessary to all social occasions. 'You seem a little bit
tired from your climb. Do come in and sit down; I am afraid that
I don't have anything apart from rum.'

Alfred thought of the whisky he had seen Barratt drink at Da
Silva. He remembered that the rum bottle was three-quarters
empty.

'Oddly,' said Mr Barratt, and it certainly was odd, 'I don't feel
like a drink. Perhaps I could have some tea?'

'Very well – tea,' said Alfred.

He went out to leave instructions to that effect for the housekeeper. Then he returned to the sitting-room, where Mr Barratt,
his mind full of tea-time thoughts, was sitting, lost in the contem-
plation of his childhood, that forgotten and happy age when
grown-ups had taken tea dressed in white flannels and tulle.

'Where did you live as a child?' Barratt asked.

'Andalusia – that was the house's name,' replied Alfred. 'It was
in Maraval. The Maraval river ran along the bottom of our
garden. Of course they have knocked it all down now and built
over it. And where did you live?'

'We lived in Scott Avenue,' said Barratt. 'The first house on
the left.'

95

'The one called the Round House?' asked Alfred, wondering if Barratt had really come all this way just to discuss the old days in this haphazard fashion.

'Yes. They haven't knocked that down yet. Someone tried to have me killed last night, you know,' he said, suddenly changing the subject without any preparation at all; it was hard to see how you could prepare anyone for such news – it was so brutal, so absurd.

'What do you mean?' asked Alfred, stupidly. A bell sounded in the hallway. 'That will be tea,' he said. He got up to go and get it.

'It is a long story,' said Barratt, when Alfred had returned and was pouring the tea. 'But you do know about this Seth person who lives in the walled house at the top of the hill?'

'Yes.'

'He sent one of his people down to shoot at my house last night …'

Alfred listened to the whole story in amazement. He wondered if Barratt was mad. He rather hoped he was; it might be less disturbing that way.

'Is there any proof that Seth is a criminal?' he asked, once the story was over. 'I mean, if the police here won't do anything, is there anything that would get the police in Port of Spain to do something?'

'There isn't a shred,' said Barratt. 'As far as I know, Seth never even leaves his house. I don't think anyone could connect him with anything illegal. The best one could do is to nail this thug Burke he has in employ. But recruiting thugs can't be difficult, and he could always get another. Everyone here is corruptible. Seth wants to use Palmer to take over Da Silva. That is his plan.'

'Palmer,' said Alfred thoughtfully. 'I am sure he wouldn't enter into any arrangement with Seth if he knew he was a criminal. Seth has never been exposed. Even Father Salvatori, the Vicar-General, has been to see him, and Mr Seth has said that he will pay for the new Cathedral more or less in its entirety. I suppose I

96

shall have to speak to Father Salvatori about what you have told me. And I shall have to speak to Simon Palmer if necessary.'

'People are easily taken in by men like Seth,' said Barratt. 'If he is allowed to build your Cathedral, there will be no end to what he can do. I think I shall go to Port of Spain for a few weeks. I shall call it sick-leave. And if and when I come back, perhaps Seth will be dead. That would be a nice Christmas present, wouldn't it? The whole thing has got to be too much for me.'

'And who will look after Da Silva while you are away?'

'Simon Palmer, of course.'

'I don't think you should go,' said Alfred hurriedly. 'The boy doesn't have the experience to deal with Seth. It would be much better for you to stay.'

'No,' said Barratt decisively. 'I need a holiday. I've been in this ghastly place for far too long already. And if Palmer is too inexperienced, Bishop, then you and Father Salvatori will have to help him, that's all.'

*

Mr Barratt, racked by deep despair, began to make his way home. When he got there he made several phone calls. One was to the head office in Port of Spain, telling them what he had decided to do. There was no objection from them. He had not had a holiday for some time. He could go away and come back in a month's time, in the New Year. The second call was to the office.

'Simon,' he said. 'I am going away. I may come back. I have spoken to the people in Port of Spain, and you are now to run the place. I suggest you go up to Seth and get that lease renewed as soon as you can. Tell him whatever you like about me – whatever he wants to hear.'

Barratt put down the phone. He wondered, as he prepared to pack, whether he would come back in the New Year. Perhaps there would be a happy ending after all, and the boy scout would deal with the monster on the top of the hill. Time would tell.

10

THE RENEWAL of the lease turned out to be simplicity itself. There was no need to tell Seth anything beyond the bare truth – that Mr Barratt had gone away on holiday and that Simon was now acting as manager of Da Silva. Simon told Seth that much when he went up to see him as arranged, after the office closed. Seth, not believing that Barratt would ever come back – for who, once warned, would be so foolish? – took the pre-prepared lease out of his wall safe; they both signed it. Thus Da Silva's lease on its San Fernando premises was renewed for another ten years on exactly the same terms as before. And that was all.

Simon was then invited to take a dip in the pool. He found a pair of trunks in the changing-room, and swam a few lengths while Seth watched from the covered seat at the side. The girl did not appear.

It was the first time he had ever seen Seth out of doors. After he had got out of the pool, as he sat there in the evening sun, he questioned Seth, trying his best not to look at his face.

'Who is that girl that I have seen here sometimes?' he asked.

'Do you like her?' asked the old man.

'Does she live here?'

'She lives here,' said Seth, feeling his question had been answered.

'Is she a relation of yours?'

'I have no relations,' said Seth. 'I suppose she does, but I am not one of her relations. You don't have any relations either, do you?'

'No, I don't,' conceded Simon, wondering at the fact that Seth had plainly taken trouble to find out about him.

'Just like me,' said Seth reflectively. 'I even have no name. Seth is my Christian name, except I don't think I was ever baptised. But I don't have a surname like other people. No one ever gave me one. Do you know where you got your surname from?'

'My mother gave it to me. She made it up, I think, because she wanted to change her own name, so no one would know her.'

'My mother,' said Seth, 'was not so inventive. I don't mind it so very much, having only one name and not two. And as for relations, I never minded not having them. If someone wants to threaten me, they have to do so directly. They can't terrorise a member of my family, because I haven't got one. No wife, no children; of course, Burke has been like a son to me. And Payne has too. Payne ain't as bright as Burke, not that that is saying much, but I have been good to them and they are loyal to me. When I die they think they'll get all this. But that isn't certain, so they are always careful. Because they aren't my children they are that little bit more grateful.'

Simon listened to this in silence.

'I suppose,' said Seth, 'that you want to have children of your own, and get married even?'

'Yes,' said Simon.

'Then that girl is not for you,' said Seth abruptly. He looked more lizard-like than ever as he said it. Simon realised that this was an attempt at a smile. 'A girl like her would ruin you. You should keep away from girls like her – I have, all my life.'

The old man said this as if he were talking of the greatest blessing of his existence. Simon wondered if the old man – and he was old, he realised, as he looked at him in the natural light of day, so withered and tortoise-like did his black skin appear: he could have been over eighty – he wondered if the old man, in addition to the missing eye, lacked other vital parts. This was not because he could not imagine a life in which passion played no part: he had never for a moment thought the clergy suffered from it, never thought what he himself felt might trouble a person like Father Salvatori or a figure like the Bishop. To some was given the grace of otherworldliness, which he imagined as a physical saintliness, an angelic disposition. But Seth, who looked like Satan himself, was surely not one of these. Seth was a man of passion, Simon thought, and if you were a man of passion then the most interesting passion of all was surely the sexual one. There was something dry and sterile about the passion for power, money and domination – so dry and sterile in fact that, if he interpreted Seth's case aright, it had dried him up completely. That was why Seth was warning him off the unnamed girl, because it was not something he himself could understand.

'There are other girls in this town,' Seth was saying. 'But not her.'

The world was indeed full of women. Simon saw them every day. But the thing was that it was only the woman he had seen by that pool-side who was the woman, rather than just any woman. No amount of warning, he realised, would put him off her. A strange thought had come into his mind: he would marry her. After all, he had been brought up as, and was, a very strict Catholic. That was in his blood. His mind had been awash with vague sexual thoughts ever since he had been twelve years old. He was now twenty-seven; he had always thought of sex as meaning marriage and, if he were to think of this girl as his future wife, that would make the pursuit of her something good.

'You be careful,' Seth was saying. 'You have got prospects, and you are intelligent. You are brighter than Burke and Payne, and you don't want to go and ruin yourself over some girl like her. Find yourself someone respectable.'

'Ruin myself?' asked Simon.

'That's what I mean,' said Seth. 'It's no use having all this' – his eyes took in the swimming-pool and the garden – 'when you can't even go out of doors, is it? I've got lots of money, but what I don't have is what you have, a kind of clean slate ...'

Simon thought of Tony Singh. Seth would always be the man who had killed, or was supposed to have killed, Tony Singh. He was, in every sense of the word, a marked man. But the girl, surely, had nothing to do with that. Tony Singh had been dead for years. Unless, of course, the old man meant that, despite his recent declaration of celibacy, the girl was in fact his daughter. That would explain her cloistered residence in his house. It would also explain his protectiveness. He wondered if the poor girl really knew what Seth, if he was her father, was like; and why she was kept out of sight. Could she know the truth, that a daughter would be an enormous liability to a gangster? She had to be kept out of it. But was it possible that this beautiful girl was the daughter of this hideous old man? It was too much like a fairy tale to be true. She was the beautiful princess he had been told about as a child, kept a prisoner in the giant's castle. And who was to rescue her but himself?

'I am not interested in her,' said Simon as casually as he could, lying through his teeth.

He wished that he knew her name; but he was afraid to ask it. If he showed too much interest in her, Seth might ensure that he never saw her again. He would have to pretend indifference.

'Well,' said Seth, 'that is just as well, for the moment.'

This seemed to be leaving a door at least ajar.

'I am glad about your promotion,' he continued. 'You've got prospects. If you're clever, and I think you are, and you don't do anything stupid, you will go far. That friend of yours, Father Salvatori: he is a clever man. I tell you that I think he will go far in the Church. I admire such men. I think I'll give you a cheque to take to him, just to show how pleased I am. It'll be another fifty-thousand dollars. He knows that I am a man to be trusted. You like Father Salvatori?'

'Yes,' said Simon.

'You respect him?'

'Yes,' said Simon, not knowing whether he did or not, but suspecting that this was what Seth wanted to hear.

'I am sure he'll tell you that I'm a man you can trust. And he'll tell you that you'll do well to listen to me. I have great respect for Father Salvatori.'

Simon wondered whether he ought to believe this or not. But the fact was that the priest seemed confident enough of Mr Seth's honesty to take his money; and, with that in mind, Simon tried to put his mind at rest.

'The only thing I want to ask you is about those six clerks,' said Seth suddenly.

'Yes,' said Simon, knowing that his was the beginning of being in Mr Seth's debt.

'They tell me that they've come back to work as if nothing has happened. I think they can't have it fairer than that. But if they give you any trouble – just let me know and I'll see that they never do it again.'

Darkness fell, as it always did, suddenly and unannounced. It was too cold to be sitting around in a wet bathing costume; while Seth went to his office to write a cheque for Father Salvatori, Simon got dressed. As he did so, he wondered about his prospects, as Seth had called them. 'You are brighter than Burke and Payne,' the old man had said, and he had spoken of them as his heirs. He wondered at the game the old man was playing, and how his daughter, if that was what she was, fitted in.

*

Simon went home. The dreariness of the place he lived in, compared with the hotel-like luxury of Seth's, brought every-day reality forcibly into his mind. He knew he was a romantic. He had always been a romantic; it was the lot of those who do not know who their fathers were, he supposed. His real father might have been a dustman, but because there was no knowing who he was, the imagination filled the gap. It was the same with the girl at Seth's. As a child, when his mother had been alive, he had sometimes wondered whether his father might not suddenly turn up one day and claim them, and that his mother was somehow waiting for him, with a patience that knew no limit in time. Had she worked in her shop day after day thinking that he would suddenly stride in and take them away to some Promised Land? And had she died of despair when she finally realised after twenty-five years that he would never come, that she could in reality wait no longer? That was the story he had invented

102

as a child; it had come as a rude shock to find, years later, that the story was a common one, because it spoke of some deep-rooted human fantasy. That was why it had spoken to him.

The truth of the matter was far more prosaic, far more like real life, and was something that he had always known: his father, if he was still alive, simply did not care about them, but had settled that account a long time ago. By looking at himself in the mirror he could tell that his father had been white; that was the reason he had never married his mother, for she was black – not very black – but black all the same. It was a horrid truth indeed to think that his parents had been separated for ever by something as accidental as the colour bar. Souls were neither black nor white – but people cared only about bodies in the real world.

But romanticism, when vanquished by truth, surfaces under another form. It changes shape. His imagination had now seized on the girl. The story he had constructed went like this: he would marry her; Seth would admit he was her father and make them his heirs; they would put his enormous wealth to good use and live happily ever after. His childhood had been *Madam Butterfly*; his manhood was now *Jack and the Beanstalk*. Yet the truth was, and he knew the truth was there, though he chose not to look it in the face, the truth was simply that he had fallen in lust with a beautiful girl about whom he knew nothing. He preferred to view the sexual act, and the acquisition of Seth's money, as some sort of elaborate fairy tale: he knew he did. That way he could think about the sin he contemplated without having to admit to himself what he was doing. Thus as he reached his flat under the cover of darkness, he could do so with a quiet mind, half sure that he was not doing anything wrong.

*

The same dark descending brought to Alfred's mind the thought that he would have to speak to Father Salvatori at dinner that night about Seth. If the man was a villain, the question about the donation towards the Cathedral would be a difficult one. It might even go

103

down as a famous scandal in ecclesiastical history if the Cathedral of San Fernando were to be built with money raised through extortion, or whatever way it was that Seth had made his money. Corruption, thought Alfred, was a terrible thing; even though it was something he had little concrete experience or idea of, he was still sure of its terribleness. But even so, there wasn't a shred of evidence, as Barratt had admitted, to incriminate Seth. It was all supposition. Seth could in fact be what Salvatori seemed to imply he was – a highly respectable man. But if one believed Barratt, where would that leave Father Salvatori? If John Salvatori were knowingly taking money from a tainted source – it was too awful to think about. But if he were doing so without realising it, in that case he would be merely naïve in the extreme. Whichever way one looked at it, Salvatori was either a fool or a knave. The only way to save the poor man's reputation was to take the view that Seth was innocent.

That there was something not altogether right about the Barratt family was something of a Palmer-Ross tradition. Alfred had heard of the family, and even known them slightly in the old days. They had had something of a reputation, and Barratt's mention of the place they had lived – the Round House in Scott Avenue – served to fix in his memory what he had heard about them as well as link those far-off Barratts of long ago with the Barratt he was dealing with now.

He supposed that he must have been too young, or away at school possibly, and that that was why he had never heard before of his brother Hugo being friendly with Barratt's sister. He now wondered what his mother and father would have thought of that. Perhaps they had heard about it and kept it from his young ears; even now he found the idea of Hugo and a Barratt together as very strange, almost incredible. His parents would have been appalled about the whole thing. If he knew them at all, they would never have countenanced a Barratt. Of course, his mother had always been very tolerant of Hugo; he had, Alfred supposed, been his mother's favourite, and a general favourite with women everywhere. Hugo had been something of a womaniser who had lived in the fast lane – quite literally; but his mother would have drawn the line at a Barratt, just as she would never have accepted one of her children marrying anyone black.

The reasons for this prejudice were many and various. Old Mr and Mrs Barratt were what used to be called 'common'. The old man had been an inspector of schools who had cultivated a slightly ridiculous interest in tropical fish. It had been rumoured by those who remembered her that his old mother had been an Englishwoman who had struggled with her aitches. This memory suddenly jolted Alfred into the realisation that his own parents had been appalling snobs. He supposed he had inherited their way of looking at the world. He too was a snob. It was an odd type of snobbery that would make you doubt Barratt's veracity purely on grounds of class. But it was snobbery, Alfred realised, that made him curse the day he had ever met Simon's mother – he had broken the bounds of chastity and class all at once. Perhaps it was the second that cost him the more.

But there were other grounds for doubting Barratt. The man was an alcoholic; alcohol could produce paranoia and persecution complexes. In addition there was also the perfectly straightforward view that alcoholics simply weren't very reliable people. That did not mean to say that Barratt had imagined the bullets crashing through his window. But it could mean that he had jumped to an unsound conclusion. Perhaps the Chief of Police had been right after all, and the bullets really had been meant for him. It was very easy to mix up houses in the dark, particularly ones of identical design. But if Barratt was right, the Chief was either very stupid indeed or aiding and abetting a criminal. Perhaps, thought Alfred, the easiest thing to do was to try to see whether the Chief of Police was an honest man or not. That would decide the case.

A sudden desire to get the thing over with, and to settle the matter without having to question John Salvatori about it, made Alfred pick up the phone. He would speak to the Chief before John came back. That was important: he did not like the prospect of being forced to question the poor young priest, of implying that he had made a serious error of judgment. God forbid. Such

105

an interview would sour everything. What that 'everything' was he did not stop to analyse. In addition the whole question of Simon Palmer was troubling him.

After a little difficulty with the operator – it was seven in the evening now, and Alfred had little experience in recent years of using the phone – he managed to contact the Chief of Police, explain who he was, and ask for his immediate presence in the Bishop's house. The Chief said he would come at once. Alfred had expected no less; he put down the phone and waited.

What, he thought, if Simon were to be the business associate of a known criminal? How much better it would be if Seth were to be as innocent as he was supposed to be rich; in that case Seth would be just the man to take a fatherly interest in the boy.

Presently the Chief of Police arrived.

Alfred had never seen the Chief before, though by happy chance the Chief had seen him, as the man was a Catholic and had been present in the Cathedral on those rare occasions that Alfred had said Mass there. He volunteered this information, and that provided a way in.

'Of course,' said Alfred, 'the Cathedral is in a terrible state and has to be rebuilt. It turns out that a certain person I don't know has given fifty-thousand dollars towards the cost of a new Cathedral. He is called Mr Seth.'

'Oh, Mr Seth,' said the Chief, speaking in the sort of tones most Catholics kept for the Holy Father.

'Now,' said Alfred, gleaning nothing from the respectful silence that followed, and forced to ask where no information was volunteered, 'What is known about Mr Seth?'

'He's a very rich man; he can well afford fifty-thousand.'

'But is he honest?' asked Alfred.

The Chief thought this a foolish, even tautologous, question. If a man gave fifty-thousand for a church to be built, that was proof of honesty.

'He is the honestest man in San Fernando,' said the Chief of Police.

'He has no criminal record?'

106

'None at all,' said the Chief stoutly. And it was true: only fools ended up with criminal records.

'And he has no criminal associations even?'

'Absolutely not,' said the Chief; for if the truth were known, no one was more associated with Mr Seth than the Chief himself, and he always thought of himself as the very embodiment of law and order.

'Well,' said Alfred uncertainly. The Chief's replies seemed certain enough, but he still had lingering doubts. He did not doubt the Chief's sincerity, but was the man perhaps a complete fool?

The Chief, sensing this uncertain pause, realising that something was hanging in the balance, decided to play his trump card. In Trinidad, personal association counted for everything, so he said:

'My first job was in Port of Spain in '48, Your Lordship.'

'Oh really?' said Alfred, recognising the allusion, for his own father had been Chief of the Colonial Police Force in Port of Spain in '48.

'I remember the Inspector and Mr Andouze very well indeed,' continued the Chief.

The scales had tipped in his favour. Clearly if the man had fond memories of the late Mr Palmer-Ross, always known as the Inspector, and Peter Andouze, who had been Alfred's godmother's husband, then he could not be all bad. In fact he struck Alfred as being good and rather simple, not dishonest at all. That became clear enough as they discussed various half-forgotten anecdotes about how the Inspector and Mr Andouze had dredged the body of Tony Singh out of the harbour in Port of Spain. As a youngster Alfred had always loved hearing about Tony Singh; but as he showed the Chief out, when their conversation was over, he knew that a certain unease persisted which even stories of famous criminals could not erase. As he waited for dinner and Father Salvatori, surrounded by the welcome aroma of chicken pilau coming from the kitchen, he knew that his unease centred on the young priest's character.

This was strange. Alfred knew that for the last twenty years he had liked no one, if by to 'like' one meant to enjoy someone's company. But he liked Salvatori. Why then did he feel a certain fear about this liking? Perhaps he did not trust Salvatori or himself. His judgment in human things had long been defective. The human heart was a most deceptive organ, unsure in judgment. Look at the mistake he had made with Simon's mother. He had deceived himself into thinking that he loved her. With Salvatori too there was also the possibility of a catastrophic mistake.

The object of his doubts came into the room, cheerful, smiling, charming and Italianate.

'Something very fortunate has happened,' he said at once. 'That is why I am a little late. But chicken pilau hardly ever can be overcooked, can it?'

'I've never cooked it myself,' said Alfred honestly, who had eaten it once a week for twenty years.

'You fry a little brown sugar to start with – but anyway, far more important than a recipe you don't want to hear is the fact that I met Simon Palmer in the street. He was just coming back from Mr Seth's. It seems he has been put in charge of Da Silva, and he was there arranging for the lease to be renewed. Anyway, it seems Mr Seth must be pleased about something, because he gave Simon a cheque to give me. Another fifty-thousand dollars.'

'It is all turning out so well,' said Alfred, catching his enthusiasm, and feeling quite odd as a result, so strange was the sensation.

'Yes, indeed,' said Alfred, as they went into dinner. 'You can tell me how to make chicken pilau. One day I might have to cook for myself.'

It was the nearest thing to a joke he had made in a long time, and Father Salvatori gave an appreciative giggle.

11

IT WAS surprising how quickly you could set to work with concrete. A week had passed and already the Cathedral bore little resemblance to its former self. Simon, passing it on his way back from work, had almost failed to recognise it. They had dug around the old building and pumped liquid concrete under its foundations, concrete made out of cement and sand imported by Da Silva, and even now, section by section, the new concrete walls were rising.

A large notice outside the building informed the unobservant of what was supposed to be taking place. A new Cathedral was being built around the old, only the new one was a strange hybrid of ancient and modern. The materials were certainly modern, but the plan was old. The illustrations showed a copy of the Basilica of Saints John and Paul in Rome, a design that Father Salvatori had hit on after a lengthy perusal of the *Michelin Guide* to Italy. The notice did not mention any architect by name, but there was a foreman, imported from Port of Spain; in addition the notice announced that construction was in the hands of Seth and Co, though it did not mention that this was a recently formed company. There were numerous illustrations; the Cathedral would have a portico. There was no dome, but a campanile was shown, clearly marked as 'Stage Two'. The old Cathedral now stood desolate amidst the building site that had engulfed it. The former Vicar-General's house had already gone, its place now a devastated area dominated by cement mixers. This then was progress, sweeping away everything that stood in its path. Construction had stopped for the evening, and when Simon went into the Cathedral all was silent. The old wood still glowed in the uncertain electric light, and the unseen termites were still eating it away; but there was an air of sadness about it, for it was a building condemned to death. It could not compete with concrete moulded in situ, designed to withstand hurricanes. The old was visibly about to give way to the new. Simon wondered that no one should question why it should necessarily do so. There were so few wooden buildings left in Trinidad now. Concrete was everywhere. Every builder in the country seemed bent on covering the island with concrete, so hard and final, in a doomed attempt to create monuments that would last. The craze had triumphed all over Port of Spain for the most part, but the monuments were hardly permanent, for just as strong was the desire to demolish what had been scarcely built; it was so easy to build in concrete, but just as easy to knock it down.

Simon sat down at the back of the church. Against the wall stood Father Salvatori's confessional, where the young priest sat awaiting penitents. It was Friday evening, and confessions were customarily heard between 5 and 6.30. As Father Salvatori was the only priest in San Fernando – no one could count the Bishop as an ordinary priest – going to confession meant going to Father Salvatori. This might have presented problems to someone other than Simon. After all, he did know the priest, and the confession box and its grille were no guarantee of anonymity. It was Father Salvatori's encouragement, he knew, that had made him acting manager of Da Silva. He had trusted Father Salvatori's judgment more than he had trusted his own, and he had ended up in Mr Seth's debt as a result. Father Salvatori was now the guiding spirit in his life, for to him he had abdicated his personal sense of responsibility. He would never have fallen in with Seth had it not been for the priest. The priest had been there throughout, a talisman of respectability. He was his conscience and, as he had trusted him so far, he would trust him in everything else as well.

As a child he had always hated being dragged off to confession by his mother once a fortnight; it had been so excruciatingly embarrassing, kneeling there in the darkness and wondering what to tell the priest on the other side of the grille. The things he knew he ought to tell he could barely force out, so awful was it to have to admit to a priest that one was only human; to do so to another human being was much easier, sometimes pleasurable even, but priests were not human, as far as Simon had been concerned. He had never thought that the distant figures on the altar actually sinned, except in the most remote sort of way. Perhaps a priest might doubt the existence of the cherubim or seraphim, but they were hardly likely to think about girls in the way a 15-year-old did, night after night.

Then he had met Father Salvatori. He did not imagine that the young Father shared his interest in sex. Far from it; in fact he was sure that Father Salvatori never thought of girls at all, being far too pure for that sort of thing. But Father Salvatori's purity (or what Simon thought was purity) didn't stretch so very far in all other directions. Father Salvatori was a friend of Seth's and, unlike the priests of his teenage years, he could not be so very morally superior to him. It was this thought, that the embarrassment would not be so excruciating – for it was Seth and not sex that troubled him now – that had made him want to go to confession, after years of not enjoying the experience.

There were other things too that had drawn him there. The confessional was a dark and secret place, a place of strict confidences, protected by the most sacred seal. Saint John Nepomucene, whoever he had been, had been done to death for refusing to divulge the secrets of the confessional. So binding was the seal of secrecy that whatever one told the priest, he was bound never to mention it again, even to the penitent. He would have to keep that secret to himself until the day he died. The burden once passed on was his forever; the secret was more hidden than if it were buried at the bottom of the sea. It was this idea that drew Simon to Father Salvatori. He wanted to pass on his burden in a situation of one-sided intimacy, as he might have done to his mother when he had been a child, but as he had never done to her or to any other living soul.

After a few moments of silence, his turn came to go in to the confessional. He could see Father Salvatori quite clearly through the grille and saw him nodding sagely as he ran through his list of sins. Simon's eyes were drawn to the shininess of his purple stole against his white shirt, which contrasted so strongly with his blond, pale face and golden hair.

The priest's eyes were shut and he seemed to be concentrating, judging by the expression on his face. His little nods seemed to indicate that he was listening, though his expression betrayed no sign of shock at what he was hearing. Simon did not know that John Salvatori was bored to death and the nods were the nods of drowsiness. He had been there an hour already and received the confidences of half a dozen old women for the most part. There was nothing that bored him more. If only he could tell all these worthy ladies the stark simple truth: he had heard it all before and each confession was more or less indistinguishable from the last. Women, at least the type who wanted to confess, bored him silly; the type who didn't want to confess were far more interesting. He often wondered about the reason for the invention of the confession box – to protect female penitents from clergy who might be aroused to breaking point by catalogues of lust – and very much doubted whether it could be true.

And now here was Simon. He had recognised the boy from the moment he had said 'Bless me Father, for I have sinned', even though he had not dared open his eyes. He supposed the boy felt he had to go to confession, and he could hardly do so to the Bishop. But even so, it was painful to hear about how someone you met socially had been 'impure in thought, word and deed'. He wondered what that well-tried phrase meant in this particular case. Perhaps one should ask those terrible questions 'Alone or with others?' and 'How many times?' But that would be too cruel. He could feel the heat coming off the box in the confined space of the confessional. He was trying to do his best not to listen.

'There are some other things that trouble me, Father,' said Simon eventually. 'I have fallen in love with a girl.'

'Is that a cause for alarm?' asked the priest impassively, yet noticing that Simon's tone had changed.

'She is no ordinary girl,' he said. 'I don't mean that she is extraordinary just because I love her,' he continued, seeing the

112

look of thin-lipped disapproval that the priest was making. He had clearly caught his full attention. 'It is her circumstances that are extraordinary. Her father is a very rich man and she lives at home with him and hardly ever seems to go out; as a result I can hardly ever see her without her father there, and I think that if he suspected what I felt he wouldn't allow me to come to the house again.'

'Then try and put her out of your mind,' said Father Salvatori a little impatiently.

'I can't.'

'Is this feeling leading you into sin?' asked the priest, anxious lest he be treated like an agony aunt, and wanting to get back to the substance of what he had heard earlier.

'Yes,' said Simon.

'Then you must drive out one passion with another,' said Father Salvatori. 'Saint Paul says it is better to marry than to burn. I suggest you find another young lady who is more suitable and marry her. I presume you are old enough to marry?' he asked, to preserve the fiction that he was dealing with an anonymous penitent. 'It's not as if you know the girl you talk about well, is it?' he added.

'I know her well enough to know that I can't find someone else just like that,' said Simon. 'And then there's all this trouble with her father.'

'Oh?' asked Father Salvatori, trying to contain his interest as best he could, but feeling that they were reaching the actual point of this story.

'I work for an import and export company. At the request of the father I have imported a shipload of cement and sand, for making concrete.'

'Yes, yes, get to the point,' said Father Salvatori impatiently – for he knew all about the making of the concrete, having discussed all that with Mr Seth.

'The trouble is that he hasn't paid me and he shows no sign of wanting to pay me at all.'

'Have you asked him to pay you?'

113

'No. He is not the sort of man you can ask things of.'

'I suppose not,' conceded Salvatori. 'But even so, I imagine some third party' – it was odd to have to refer to oneself in this way – 'some third party has paid him for the concrete materials, haven't they? And so all he has to do is pass the money he has received on to you. Now why shouldn't he do so?'

'That is precisely it, Father. He has been given the money for the cement and sand by the third party but he hasn't paid me for them, so he's effectively sold what wasn't his and is keeping the money. Now either I can write it off as a bad debt, which will be hard as it is at least a hundred thousand dollars, or else I can hide the loss by falsifying the accounts. Whatever I do, he has effectively robbed my company. And as I am in love with his daughter and daren't offend him, I really don't know what I can do.'

'I see,' said Father Salvatori thoughtfully.

Indeed he did see. Seth had deceived him. The old man had given him a hundred thousand dollars; this same amount had been paid to the company he had set up, Seth and Co, which was to do the construction at cost price. But Seth was milking Da Silva and would get the building materials for free, by the simple expedient of not paying for them. Thus the diocese would get a Cathedral, Seth would get back his hundred-thousand-dollar donation, minus whatever he had to pay his workers, and Da Silva would foot the major part of the bill. In fact when you remembered the other monies that were flowing in and which would go to Seth and Co, Seth would get his money back with interest. In addition he would have gained the goodwill of the site workers, as true a bunch of thugs as ever Father Salvatori had seen.

'I could stop the order to import more cement and sand in the future,' said Simon, interrupting the silence.

'Oh, don't do that,' said the priest, his mind suddenly picturing the hideous spectacle of a half-built Cathedral. 'You see,' he continued, more calmly now, working the thing out, 'you have done nothing wrong. It is all the fault of your client. He is the one who is dishonest. You must simply leave the account as it is –

114

unpaid. I know that means that your company will in effect be giving him a free loan, but you will just have to hope that eventually he will pay you. And really, as you haven't brought the subject up with him, you can't be sure that he does in fact not intend to pay you, however much you may suspect him of being dishonest. Perhaps if you try and win his confidence he may pay you and let you see his daughter as well. Give him time.'

Simon said that he would follow this advice.

'Good,' concluded the priest. 'And for the other things, say three Hail Marys as your penance.'

The words of absolution followed. Simon felt that his burden of guilt had now been taken away, and was now the property of someone else. He went on his way rejoicing.

Father Salvatori dealt with the remaining penitents more quickly than he might have done, for something of a backlog had developed while he had been occupied with Simon; then he locked up the Cathedral, still in a perturbed frame of mind. All this was very bad of Mr Seth. He had never expected it. He supposed that Mr Seth was using the building of the Cathedral to launder money, or rather what he imagined people meant by laundering money. He made a huge charitable donation to the Church, exempt from tax, and then got it all back again via Seth and Co. He should have realised something like this was afoot, and never allowed the man to undertake the construction.

But as he stepped out into the street, his perturbation evaporated. They were at least gaining a Cathedral out of the swindle. And it was Seth who was the criminal, not Father Salvatori. So, consoled by his rising concrete walls, and thinking that evil would come out of good, he made his way into the town. The workmen had only been at work for a week; incredible as it seemed, another two weeks might even see the completion of the shell. That was a comforting thought. As for Simon Palmer, that was not an insoluble problem. Something could be done. He had never heard of such a person as Seth's daughter up to now, but he was determined to know more. For he knew that even the sexual urge could be harnessed to a good end, if one knew the right way to go about it. Thus he had made up his mind to call on Simon, to strike while the iron was hot, and not go back to the Bishop's house at once.

*

He rang the bell of the flat where Simon lived and was admitted with something like surprise.

'I was just passing,' he said breezily. 'I knew where you lived and thought I'd make a little pastoral visit to you before I went back for supper. Perhaps you have got some drink in the house?'

'I have a little bit of whisky in the kitchen,' said Simon.

'Whisky? What luxury,' said the priest. 'All the Bishop stocks is rum, which may be plentiful and cheap, but I find it dull, dull, dull.'

This seemed to invite Simon into a conspiracy of indiscretion.

'I have had lunch with the Bishop,' he volunteered from the 'kitchen', which was in truth just one wall of the sitting-room.

'I know,' said Salvatori. 'He told me. But I can't imagine what you talked about.'

'I can't remember,' said Simon, pouring out the drinks. 'I think we talked about general topics, what I was doing, that sort of thing. It was a little awkward.' Salvatori made no reply, so he felt it only polite to continue. 'I mean it was awkward in the sense that we didn't have anything really to talk about. I am just the son of a shopkeeper, and he is ... well ... he is Alfred Palmer-Ross.'

'Yes. The Palmer-Rosses are what people call a good family. But I think the Bishop is a very shy man,' said Salvatori thoughtfully. 'What is strange is that he has absolutely nothing to be shy about. He was born into a family where everyone was at least someone. He was someone from the day he was born. And when he became a priest it was assumed he would be a Bishop right from the start. And yet here he is, hiding himself away. Some years ago people used to say that he ought to be the Archbishop and not Alphonsus. He's like one of those men who have killed someone in a duel or by accident, and have to lie low for the rest of their lives. But it is very odd, when you think of all those advantages he has had. You and I never had anything handed to us on a plate, and look how well we have done for ourselves.'

'But perhaps the Bishop's advantages were in fact disadvantages, Father,' said Simon.

'You must call me John,' said Salvatori. 'No one does except the Bishop. I've heard people say that when you are privileged you can never quite get over it. I've never heard such rubbish. People who say that just want to make others feel sorry for them. I can't understand how being born rich and famous could ever hurt you. Everything I have got, I have worked for; everything I have got, I have received from the Church. My parents weren't anyone special. My grandfather came here from Italy as a pastry cook.' He leaned back with his whisky, contemplating how far he had come. His eyes travelled around the room, taking in its cheerless discomfort. Then he said, as if it were the most natural thing in the world: 'I can't think why you don't get married, Simon.'

Simon, who was now seeing a more human and less clerical side of Father Salvatori's nature, was suddenly reminded that he had confessed to him barely half an hour before. He felt his skin burn with embarrassment.

'This place could do with a woman's hand,' said Salvatori, pretending not to notice his discomfort. 'And the thing is that you could marry whoever you want to, as you don't have any relatives who could object to your choice. And I am sure Da Silva must be paying you enough, now that you are running the place.'

'I am better off than I have ever been,' he admitted.

'And everyone knows that you are good-looking; I can't think what you are waiting for.'

'Perhaps I haven't met anyone I like enough?' said Simon.

'That is true,' said the priest. 'I would like it so much if you were to marry some nice rich girl. An heiress. Do you know any heiresses?'

'There is always Mr Seth's daughter,' said Simon at last.

'I didn't know he had one,' said Salvatori. 'I always thought he was childless. That was one of the reasons I thought he had taken such a liking to you.'

'I think she is his daughter.'

'Then if he has a daughter, you must marry her,' said the priest. 'On a more practical note,' he said, changing his tone, 'why don't you and I go up there tomorrow morning and use the swimming-pool? He did say that we could go whenever we liked, didn't he?'

'We wouldn't necessarily see the girl,' said Simon.

'Oh, the girl,' said Salvatori, as if he had already lost interest in her. 'Don't worry about her. If you really want to see her, I'll ask Mr Seth to let you. There aren't many doors that are closed to priests, and there are none that have ever been closed to this one.'

'You seem to be taking a lot of trouble over this,' said Simon.

'Perhaps I am,' said Salvatori. 'It may be my natural desire to help people. I'd like to sit by a pool tomorrow; I feel worn out. I think I'd better go back to the Bishop now. He likes to talk to me before dinner in the evenings. He doesn't like my being late.'

'But you said that he was very shy,' said Simon.

'He is with everyone except me,' said Salvatori happily. 'You see doors do open to me. At least, I have never met a shut one yet. I think he trusts me. Perhaps one day he will tell me his secret.'

'Has he a secret? I didn't know.'

'Of course you didn't. That is why it is a secret,' said Father Salvatori with a giggle, for the whisky was going to his head. Generally whisky went to his legs and made them rubbery and heavy; but for some reason, perhaps because of the company of Simon, he felt quite light-headed. 'He has a secret sadness,' he continued. 'I'd love to know what it is, wouldn't you?'

'Yes, I suppose I would. Everyone has a secret, and if you find out what it is you begin to understand them. I must say I am puzzled by the Bishop; he seems to take so much trouble over me – I mean he invited me to lunch – but when I got there ...'

'And what is my secret, do you know that?' asked Salvatori, with the egotism typical of the tipsy.

'I can guess it,' said Simon, giving him a level look, as he refilled his glass, the type of look that made the priest feel suddenly more sober. 'Your secret is the fact that you have low origins, or what some people would call low origins. It explains your ambitions, the fact that your grandfather was a pastry cook.'

'And what about you?' said the priest. 'At least I know who my ancestors were.'

Simon smiled and said, 'That is quite right; but that uncertainty is rather better than the certainty that they were pastry-cooks.'

'When I am a Bishop I am going to have a rolling-pin on my coat of arms,' said Salvatori seriously.

'And do you often think about being a Bishop?' asked Simon.

Once again Salvatori sensed that the conversation was wandering into dangerous territory. Ambition was supposed to be something of a sin; he did in fact want to be a Bishop; his whole life so far had aimed towards that consummation; there was hardly a moment when he didn't think that one day he would be a Bishop – and his most dreadful fear was that one day he would not be a Bishop, because somehow he would be found out. Was this boy Simon about to find him out? There was a danger. Realising that there was truth in wine, he virtuously put down his glass and resolved to change the subject. They would talk about the Bishop instead; they had been talking about him until he himself had interrupted Simon.

'I think the Bishop has a secret,' he said. 'And it is nothing to do with social origin or anything like that. Everyone knows about his family and where he was born and where he comes from. His secret is something much more private and personal. It is a sort of sadness that he carries around with himself.'

'Do many priests carry around terrible secret sadnesses?' asked Simon, filled with curiosity.

'Some people would say that they all do,' said Salvatori, for

119

once telling the truth. 'In time these things all come out. There may be something that makes him think he is unworthy to be a Bishop, but ...'

The thought of clerical unworthiness was something that Salvatori found rather unsettling. Perhaps it was dangerous to get into this sort of conversation. One might find oneself telling confidences that one might later regret. Of course, he wasn't drunk, but he was beginning to think that he wasn't quite making sense. He rose to go.

'I mustn't be late for dinner,' he said. 'And I hope he doesn't smell the whisky on my breath. I'll see you tomorrow; don't forget.'

*

Father Salvatori hurried off into the night, no longer drunk, for the night air was refreshing; but he still had that thrill of excitement about him, that thrill of fear that comes to anyone who plays a part and allows himself to relax for a moment. He was a man who, from the very earliest days of his clerical career, had always been on his guard, ready with the answers that were expected of him, and cautious lest what he really felt should slip out by accident. Tonight he had rather let the mask of discretion slip for an instant or two. One of the truths that had almost emerged was the fact that, despite his reverential behaviour towards him, he did not hold Alfred Palmer-Ross in breathless respect. On the contrary, he thought him a bit of a fool. Monsignor Palmer-Ross could have been Archbishop of Port of Spain if he had set his mind to it – on paper at least he was far better qualified for the job than Nourganian had ever been. Or else he could have risen high in the Vatican diplomatic service, if he had bothered to use his gifts in that direction. But he had thrown it all away. John Salvatori thought that if he had been born rich and upper-class nothing would have held him back and he would not have stopped until he had become Pope. He certainly wouldn't have chosen to remain in San Fernando. God forbid.

He had already decided that San Fernando should be no more

than a stepping-stone on the way to something better. He would stay for two years and then go back to Port of Spain. He could only imagine staying on in San Fernando for longer if he were given Palmer-Ross's job; but that was unlikely as Palmer-Ross was years away from retirement, hardly seemed willing to move and did not seem about to die either. But despite his dislike of the place, it was not to be sniffed at. He was already making his mark, doing well for himself. Mr Seth valued him, and Mr Seth, however he had got his money, was the richest and most important man in the town. The new Cathedral would do the name of Salvatori a power of good. It would be one of the biggest churches in Trinidad. It would certainly be the newest. People would notice him because of it. And if he got Simon Palmer married off to Seth's daughter – or at least appeared to smooth the path for him – what a coup that would be. Simon would be grateful; and, when Seth was dead, he would be rich.

It was not that John Salvatori was greedy; he rarely thought about money and the comforts it brought. Those thoughts were for his leisure moments, when there was nothing better to think of. The real business of clerical life lay in implementing what was called 'the spirit of Vatican Two'. This, he knew, would be anathema to Alfred Palmer-Ross, but as the Bishop was taking no interest at all in the new Cathedral, and had not visited the site, there was no need to fear his objections, which, if they were made at all, would be made when it was too late. You couldn't argue with concrete once it had set, just as you couldn't rebuild a demolished Cathedral. The Bishop would be faced with a *fait accompli*; one morning he would see a Vatican Two, in the spirit of, Cathedral. He might notice it from his verandah and choke over his rum punch. Gone would be the old wooden altar, the confession box, the dark mysterious ambience. Out of their ashes would arise, and was already arising, something as new and as comfortless as a nuclear shelter. Of course, it was a copy of Saints John and Paul in Rome, but a copy made in the neo-brutalist style. There would be rough undressed concrete, cold unwelcoming glass and harsh neon lighting: something like a cross between a power-station and an abattoir.

In point of fact, John Salvatori's own taste in things ecclesiastical was rather florid. He had a penchant for incense and vestments, lace and bells. But he was prepared to sacrifice his own preferences; the truth was that these things were out of date. Trying to retain the old would not get you noticed. To be a mover and a shaker meant that nowadays you had to be a wrecker. It was the only way to get on.

*

He was slightly late, and dinner was waiting for him when he arrived. He was fulsome in his apologies.

'I was visiting Simon Palmer,' he explained. 'I was kept slightly longer than I expected.'

'You seem to be quite friendly with him,' observed Alfred. 'Anyway,' he continued, 'let me help you to some souse. It's a special treat.'

'How lovely,' murmured Salvatori, as the Bishop kindly put a pig's trotter onto his outstretched plate.

12

THE NEXT MORNING Alfred was in the room he used as his study. It was nine o'clock. He had been up since before six, had spent an hour in his private chapel at prayer and then said Mass. Father Salvatori had joined him for the hour's meditation, and then gone to the Cathedral to celebrate the daily Mass there. He had said nothing about returning for breakfast, and subsequently Alfred had breakfasted alone, just as he had said Mass alone. Now, having said the bulk of his breviary for the day, his well-practised tongue having run through the Latin with ease, he sat in his study, ready to fill in the three hours that remained before lunch. There were various pieces of correspondence that demanded his attention. He was constantly being sent inquisitive questionnaires, impersonally composed, from anonymous people who worked for such bodies as the World Council of Churches, asking him about things like evangelisation. He had begun to think that it might be amusing to pass them on to John Salvatori, who was clearly far more up to date on these things than he was. In addition to the humdrum routine matters that took up so much of his time, he was filling in his spare hours writing an article on the history of relations between the State of Israel and the Holy See. This was the sort of subject that appealed to him; it was obscure but one day might be important. His approach was very meticulous, and when the article was finished, he thought of sending it to the editor of the *Tablet*. In the past he had been in the habit of writing articles for the *Clergy Review*. A few of them had become minor classics, especially a series that dealt with grounds for nullity of marriage, which had been photocopied and kept for reference by numerous seminarians grappling with the details of Canon Law. But his best work, much to his shame, was a learned article that had appeared some years before, nearly twenty in fact, entitled 'The Pastoral Role of the Bishop, as envisaged by the Second Vatican Council'. This article had enjoyed modest fame as it acted as a summary of all the Council had said about bishops, and did so exhaustively and lucidly. This was always a matter for shame for Alfred, that he should know what Bishops were supposed to do, and yet do it so little himself.

This morning he should have been putting the finishing touches to his article on Israel and the Holy See. But as was often the case with a project that has lost its initial lustre, he could not quite settle to the work; instead he turned to a book he had been thinking about for some time. It was one of those heavy and old-fashioned black-bound volumes about the churches of Rome, a book he had first bought when he had been a student in Italy. He looked up the section on the Basilica of Saints John and Paul. Of course, he remembered the place well, but he wanted to have a clearer idea in his head about its exact dimensions. Unfortunately, the book was an Italian one and spoke of metres. Alfred had as little idea about metres as he had about evangelisation – he knew what they were, but could never quite visualise them – so he was thrown back on to that less reliable measure, memory. He supposed the church would seat four hundred people with ease. That would make it just the right size for the new Cathedral. He was, on reflection (for he never quite approved of changing the status quo), rather pleased about the whole idea of copying a Roman Church. As far as he could remember, Saints John and Paul was rather a pleasant church; even the black-and-white photograph in the book looked quite cheerful. Perhaps something beautiful would be born in San Fernando after all. He now thought that, left to himself, John would not have much by way of taste – people in Trinidad very rarely did. It was thus a reassurance to know that the church being built was a copy. One could not go wrong with a copy.

It struck him that this paternalistic spirit of indulgence that he felt towards John and his new Cathedral was a sign of his lack of confidence that he felt in the young priest – or would 'esteem' be a better word? That was why he was so happy to have him as Vicar-General: John was a second-class sort of fellow, though a very good one at that, and thus he was no real rival. How odd, thought Alfred: here I am in San Fernando, and yet I am afraid of rivals. It only went to show how strange human nature was, if it could be possessive over something which was not in itself desirable. But all the same, he feared rivals. A rival meant someone who was as good as yourself, someone who was your equal. Alfred Palmer-Ross disliked his equals. He never saw members of his own family; and he hardly ever saw Simon Palmer, who despite his mother's blood, was the nearest person to him in the world. He knew he had neglected that boy. Perhaps he ought to go and see him. But it was Saturday and Da Silva would be closed.

These thoughts were interrupted by the ringing of the telephone. This event, in itself unusual, shattered his reflections. He picked up the receiver.

'Alfred,' said a voice.

'Oh, Your Grace,' he replied, for he recognised Nourganian's voice and only the Archbishop ever called him Alfred. 'You seem to be phoning me rather a lot recently.'

'This is the second time in twenty years,' said Nourganian. 'However, you are quite right: using the telephone can become quite addictive, I believe. It is rather nice to think of someone and be able to speak to them directly and immediately. I was just wondering about how John Salvatori was getting along.'

'But you already know,' said Alfred. 'I mean, he submitted the whole project about the new Cathedral to you, didn't he? And the work has already begun. I haven't been down to see it myself, but John keeps me informed, you know.'

'Does he? I am not really interested in architecture,' said the wily Armenian. 'I am far more interested in people.'

'Oh, he seems to be very happy. He is certainly busy enough. I must say he has been quite a breath of fresh air in this place.'

'I am so glad to hear it. I knew he would be, and I did hope that

125

you would take to him. Evidently you have. San Fernando will do him good too, after Port of Spain.'

'I never liked Port of Spain so very much myself,' observed Alfred.

'John did,' said Nourganian. 'He liked it a great deal, though not as much as he liked Rome. I do think he is an able young man, don't you? I mean, he's barely arrived in San Fernando and already he's started to build a new Cathedral, and he's organised all the finances, and we can trust him to finish the job. Many people would say that he's just the sort of young man – though he's almost forty now – whom we need as a Bishop. Now what do you think of that?'

Nourganian had spoken as if he were discussing the selection process for the next test match. Alfred was silent. It had never occurred to him that Salvatori was marked out for promotion in just the way he had been. The idea took him completely by surprise. Who could be so stupid as to imagine Salvatori as a Bishop?

'Oh no,' he said at last. 'I mean, he is a very nice young man, and he's good at organising things and he is very pleasant company; I imagine he has always been a success with the people, because he is very likeable, but Our Lord didn't choose his Apostles because they were good at running things, did he?'

'What do you mean?' asked Nourganian.

'I suppose I mean that he's not like my idea of a Bishop,' said Alfred. 'I really can't believe that you are serious in thinking of making him one. I mean, he is a nice chap and all that, but is he, well, religious enough?'

'I have never heard that mentioned as a qualification before now,' said Nourganian. 'As for being serious, well, it is serious, but perhaps not as serious as you think. And at the same time it is being floated. You see, John was always very good with the Papal Nuncio ...'

Alfred winced.

'Now tell me,' said Nourganian. 'How is my unofficial godson, Simon Palmer? That is a much more pleasant topic, I am sure.'

'I was just thinking of going to see him,' said Alfred, who found the topic a slightly uncomfortable one. 'He is acting Manager of Da Silva now. Perhaps you know his home address, though.'

'Yes, I do. It is No. 2, Henderson Avenue. They do give the roads silly names. Oh well, happy visiting, and do give my regards to John Salvatori. I am glad he's such a comfort to you. Good-bye.'

'Good-bye,' said Alfred.

This telephone call was a sufficient catalyst to persuade Alfred to go down to the town at once and call on Simon Palmer. He did not know whether the news that there were a few foolish people, among them the Papal Nuncio, who seemed to think John Salvatori ought to be a Bishop, had anything to do with his sudden desire somehow to make up for not paying enough attention to Simon earlier. He did not stop to think whether the attention he had lavished on Salvatori had been merited or not; rather he decided to go and see Simon, ostensibly to pass on Alphonsus Nourganian's regards, which was the ideal excuse.

He went into the hall and left a note for the housekeeper, saying that he had gone out, should anyone call – not that anyone ever did call. Then he walked down the hill to Henderson Avenue, and luckily his path did not take him past the Cathedral. He half-thought of making a detour to inspect the work in progress, but told himself that a week's work would hardly be worth seeing. Besides, he had put off seeing Simon for long enough. Thus he hurried off towards Henderson Avenue, not turning aside to anything.

*

No. 2 turned out to be part of the only two-storeyed house in the entire road. The number was painted on the gate that shut off an external staircase, which led up to the first floor. Alfred opened the gate and went up.

He found himself on a broad terrace. There was some old cane furniture there, the type that one need not bother to put away, because it was not worth anyone's while to steal. He called out Simon's name, but instinctively he knew that he wasn't there; there was an atmosphere of desertion about the place. He advanced along the terrace and looked into the flat through the large glass doors. The place was somewhat untidy, but he supposed that was normal with young men who lived alone. He noticed an empty whisky bottle on the formica table and two unwashed glasses. There did not seem to be any books lying around, nor even any magazines. He wondered about the whisky; then he remembered that John must have been there last night. That explained the two glasses. In fact he now seemed to remember that he had smelt whisky last night when John Salvatori had come into supper; perhaps that was why he had not had much of an appetite for a second helping of souse.

He sat down on one of the uncomfortable cane chairs. It creaked menacingly. A terrible sense of sadness and loss swept over him. For a moment he felt close to tears. To look through that window was to look into a life so different from his own. There was no sense of comfort here. He did not suppose that Simon was unhappy; in fact he was sure he was quite content with life, which made the whole thing the more sad. Here was this boy, his son, content with so little. He ought to do something. For a moment he almost regretted the fact that he had stayed a priest and a bishop. If he had done the impossible and brought the boy up, married his mother, how different Simon's life would have been. He would not have ended up in this awful place, San Fernando. The view from the balcony of a dusty road and ramshackle architecture was hardly consoling. But Simon would never have known it if he had been Alfred's acknowledged son. It was quite true that he was of mixed race; but no one would even have noticed that in England, for example. In England he would merely have passed for dark and handsome. But this was the saddest thing in the world – what might have been.

At last Alfred got up, rousing himself. If Simon were not at home, then he would be at Da Silva. He would go and see. In all probability he was at work, even on a Saturday morning.

128

He left Henderson Avenue and walked towards the port. Soon, too soon, it would be Christmas. This was a depressing thought. Thank God Christmas came but once a year. In Trinidad it came amidst a blaze of sunshine, at the very height of the tourist season. You could swim in Maracas Bay on Christmas Day itself – many did – and feel no sense of incongruity about it. Christmas did not really work any more, thought Alfred, in tropical climes. God alone knew what it must be like in Australia. In England, that far-off country he carried in his blood, but of which he knew practically nothing, in England he imagined they still celebrated Christmas with a degree of success. It was the cold weather: when the religious element failed, you could always rely on the ingrained paganism of the northern races. They could always celebrate the winter solstice as their ancestors the Druids had done.

He wondered how all his mother's friends who had gone to live in London celebrated Christmas. Most of them seemed to live in Battersea and South Kensington. His own memory of London was now vague; the only thing he could remember with clarity was the freezing cold. But perhaps if you lived in such a cold place, you could imagine how shepherds had watched their flocks by night, shivering on the ground. Sheep and shepherds would make sense. But to try and imagine it in Trinidad seemed hopeless. The magic did not work any more. You were left with a sense of guilty dissatisfaction as you stared at your expensive artificial Christmas tree. What could you do? You could hardly give up the effort altogether and say that the twenty-fifth of December was simply another ordinary day. It hadn't always been like this. Years ago, the problem had not existed.

The cicadas might have made their noise the night long outside the churches at midnight, under a tropical moon, but the miracle of Christmas had been there. He remembered it. The miracles had been conveyed in strange yet familiar words, the words of the Mass. But that language had now disappeared and they were left with everyday words that sounded just like themselves. To sound like oneself was very bad indeed – for if this world was all that was left to them, how on earth were they to speak of God?

Uneasy at the thought of the approaching feast, and disturbed at the impoverishment of his faith, Alfred arrived at Da Silva. He found one solitary clerk in charge.

'I would like to see Mr Palmer,' he said.

'The Acting Manager,' said the boy, investing the title with all the dignity that his voice could command, 'ain't here.'

'Oh,' said Alfred. (Why did he preface everything he said with 'Oh'? Was it the result of twenty years' diffidence?) 'I have been to his house. Do you know where he might be?'

'That I do,' said the clerk, who had been brought up to trust the clergy. 'He has gone to Mr Seth's house with the other minister.'

'Minister,' thought Alfred: 'the other minister'. He turned and left the office. It was odd how little he knew about Simon or John. Of course, they had known each other in Port of Spain, long before he had known either of them. How well they had known each other he had never before bothered to consider. He had never thought to think about it. It was a novel thought. Equally novel was the strange feeling that was creeping over his body as he stood there on the pavement; he did not recognise it at first, and wondered if he were becoming ill. Then he realised that this unaccustomed feeling was the onset of jealousy.

*

Father Salvatori was relaxing by the pool-side. Life in San Fernando was not so very bad after all. He had a rum-and-Coke in one hand, given to him by Seth himself. They had been discussing the merits of souse. Father Salvatori could not understand how anyone would want to eat pigs' trotters boiled with peppers; but Seth had spoken for some time about the benefits of souse, and was now half way through an anecdote about his mother, which Father Salvatori was doing his best to follow. He thought he was getting more used to the man's missing eye, but he still did his best to avoid looking at him

130

too much, preferring to look at what Simon was up to in the pool, while pretending to concentrate on the rather involved anecdote about the old man's mother, who, if Salvatori guessed aright, was no better than she ought to have been.

This sitting together in the shade was the beginning, they both supposed in their different ways, of an alliance, even familiarity. There was an unspoken understanding between them. Each knew the other. And Salvatori knew something Seth did not: namely, that he would never be able to denounce the old fraud-ster because the knowledge of his guilt was protected by the seal of the confessional. He would never be able to breathe to a living soul that Seth was a thief; Seth was safe with him. And John Salvatori knew that he was safe with Seth.

For Mr Seth was very happy to be entertaining the priest. There was something particularly satisfying in the knowledge that this priest had called unannounced and more or less unin-vited; the priest was courting his company. It made him feel respectable. Respectability was something he had undervalued in the past. As a young man he had wanted to be feared, but now as he grew older – and he felt his age more and more – he wanted the comfort and shelter of the law. For that reason he had spent so much time and money conciliating the Chief of Police, and at the same time doing his best to restrain the more violent enter-prises of Burke and Payne. There was no point, he was coming to realise, in being very rich and yet having to live in the constant fear that what you had done to others might soon be done to you. He wanted a way out. And here was the priest come to provide it. Once the Cathedral was built, his reputation, his new reputa-tion that is, would be made. He would be a civic worthy, a benefactor of the town and the Church, and not just the sinister man who lived on the hill. He no longer wanted to be feared; he now wanted to be loved as well. And as for his money, that like his reputation was going to be laundered, thanks to the co-operation of Da Silva.

Father Salvatori, in a fit of clerical modesty, had declined to undress and jump in the pool, despite the offer of swimming

131

trunks, but he had rolled up his sleeves and undone the top button of his shirt. He was not the athletic type. His arms were yellow-skinned and pudgy. White men won few gold medals at the Olympics, thought Seth. This man was almost eager to accept client status – how different from the white men he had known in his youth.

'Would you like to ask me a favour?' said Seth, in his expansive mood.

'You have a daughter, I hear,' said Salvatori, by way of preparation.

'Oh no,' said Seth. 'I am childless.'

'But there is a girl living here, in this house, isn't there? Simon has seen her.'

'That is perfectly true,' said Seth. 'He has seen her here and I told him she wasn't my daughter. But please ask me whatever you like. I like it when people ask me favours, especially ones I am able to perform. Ask me to do something for you; let me give you something.'

'I am in your debt already. You are building a Cathedral for me.'

Seth merely smiled.

'I want to ask something for Simon,' said the priest. 'He tells me that he wants to meet this girl. He says that you seem to keep her locked away and out of sight. It is not an unnatural request for a young man like him to make.'

'I hoped it was a request he wouldn't make,' said Seth. 'I told him no good would come of it.'

'What harm could it do?' asked Salvatori, wondering if the old man was something of a prude. 'I mean, Simon is a very respectable young man, and very virtuous.'

Seth knew exactly what harm it could do, and to whom.

'I'll give him anything he wants,' he said at length. 'If he stays to lunch he can meet her then. She is a good girl and she will do as I tell her. And as for Simon, I think he will be grateful, won't he?'

'Oh, indeed yes,' said Salvatori.

'I'll tell Burke and the other one to drive you back to the Bishop's for lunch and then I'll send them off to Port of Spain,' said Seth. 'That way they'll be out of the way until four at least.'

Father Salvatori thought that these were rather elaborate arrangements, but that it might be construed as indelicate to point that out. Simon was surely not going to need the whole house to himself to get friendly with this girl.

Simon got out of the pool; Father Salvatori gave him a nod to signify that the business was done. Then wrapping a towel around himself, Simon came and joined them in the shade.

'Soon it will be Christmas,' said Father Salvatori.

'I wonder what all the Muslims and Hindoos will do?' asked Seth. 'How will they mark the birth of the Prince of Peace?'

It was last Christmas that a group of terrorists had stormed the Parliament building and shot the Prime Minister; it was a topic that few cared to discuss.

'The Hindoos are very well-behaved people,' said Father Salvatori with almost colonial benevolence. 'As for the Muslims ...'

'They are a bunch of no-good men,' said Seth sententiously. 'I thank the Lord I am a Christian.'

'Are you?' asked Simon.

'I would have thought it was obvious,' said the old Cyclops. 'I have taken up virtue in my old age and put off the indiscretions of my youth; just like that man in the Bible.'

Which man in the Bible wasn't clear, but Father Salvatori did not feel that it was incumbent on him to raise the point.

'I have enjoyed myself,' he said, getting up. 'And now I must go. The Bishop always has his lunch at twelve sharp.' He put his hand on Simon's shoulder to hold him in his chair.

Seth accompanied the priest towards the house. Simon was left on his own, and in a few moments he heard the sound of a car being started up. Then Seth returned.

'I've sent them all away,' he said. 'Burke and Payne and the Father. Burke and Payne are going to Port of Spain to look at some imitation marble I have it in mind to buy and then to see a

133

few people. They will be gone until late.' He sat down in mid-explanation, and sighed. 'Do you like Burke and Payne?' he asked.

'No,' said Simon, who had decided that honesty with Seth was always the best policy.

'Why not?'

'They frighten me.'

'Good. That is as it should be. I wouldn't like you to like them at all.'

'Why not?'

'Burke,' said Mr Seth, 'is a murderer.'

*

'Well,' said the Bishop, when he sat down to luncheon with Father Salvatori fifteen minutes later, 'I gather you have been visiting our most important parishioner – our benefactor, in fact. I found out quite by accident. Don't be alarmed. Actually I didn't think I would mention it to you. It is just that I am rather curious about Mr Seth. I'd like you to tell me about him. I'm eaten away with vulgar curiosity.'

This last declaration was certainly true. He was curious – but not about Mr Seth. He was curious about John Salvatori and Simon. There seemed to be a whole secret life there of which he knew nothing.

'Oh, he is a very hospitable man,' said Salvatori. 'He is the sort who likes doing favours for people. The whole Cathedral thing is fixed, by the way. He told me that I didn't need to worry about the money side of things at all. There was another reason I went up there and that was because of Simon Palmer. He's got it into his head that he must marry Mr Seth's daughter.'

'But that is impossible,' said Alfred.

'He is twenty-seven,' said Salvatori. 'I think it's strange he hasn't married already. But as you rightly say, it is impossible, for the simple reason that Seth has no daughter, or so he says. But there is a beautiful black girl living in the house whom Simon thinks is Seth's daughter. He may of course be right – an illegitimate daughter probably, whom Seth won't acknowledge for obvious reasons.'

'What obvious reasons?'

'I suppose a rich man with no other relatives may not want to expose his only child to fortune-hunters. Someone, though, will have to inherit his fortune. And these people always like to have secrets.'

'Has he got a fortune?'

'They say it's vast.'

'And does Simon Palmer want to get his hands on it?'

'I should think so,' said Salvatori, after a moment's consideration. 'I can't believe he is passionately in love with her. I think it must be the money.'

This was indeed what Father Salvatori thought. Seth was defrauding Da Silva and Simon had to get the money back somehow. On top of that, Salvatori found it impossible to imagine anyone being in love with an unknown black girl. Being a man of low motives himself, he had fallen into the habit of assuming that other people were of low motives too. However, these were hardly things he could explain to the Bishop; so, when asked why he thought this way, he merely said, 'Instinct.'

There was silence for a moment, while they both helped themselves to the dish of pastelles in front of them. Father Salvatori was finding the food produced by the housekeeper rather hard to cope with; he wished Seth had invited him to lunch, and fed him on imported steak. Pastelles were all very well in theory, but he found it rather hard to chew banana leaf stuffed with corn meal, and the difficulty it involved certainly precluded conversation for the time being. He watched Monsignor Palmer-Ross chewing his pastelle with an abstracted expression on his face; clearly the Bishop didn't care what he was eating: he was too curious about Simon Palmer. It occurred to Salvatori's Italian mind that the poor man might well be mad, that his mind had been turned by twenty years' residence in San Fernando and a diet of souse, pastelles and goat curry.

'But I don't understand,' said Alfred, trying to hide his dismay.

'I don't understand why you went up to see Seth. If Simon Palmer wants to marry this girl – what has that got to do with you?'

'Well,' said Salvatori, alarmed by something in the Bishop's tone, and wondering if he'd have to go over all these lies again one day, and scared lest he be detected in inconsistency, 'Simon thought that I could persuade Seth to let him see the girl.'

'And did you?'

'Yes. It wasn't hard; my intervention wasn't really necessary.'

'But I still don't see why you should want to see Simon Palmer married off to this girl,' said Alfred a little querulously.

'I am not free to speak,' said Salvatori, using the usual phrase to denote the seal of confession.

Silence fell again; the conversation could not be continued; the subject could hardly be referred to again. Alfred helped himself to another pastelle – really, food was the only luxury he allowed himself – and wondered how black Seth's daughter would be. But it was hopeless trying to put a brave face on it. The whole situation was irremediably disastrous. It was terrible to think that Simon might come under the influence of a man like Seth forever. Once done, it could never be undone. He would be more like his mother and not at all like his father. He would be lost entirely.

Not for the first time he wondered if he should not cut the Gordian knot, and tell the boy who he was. He could ask him to come up to the Bishop's house and tell him that he was his father. But as soon as he tried to imagine himself saying those words his mind baulked at the very idea. He could not do it. He could not admit to the boy who was, thanks to Archbishop Nourganian, a pious Catholic, that he had failed as a priest and that he was the result of that failure. Those words, that admission of guilt, were quite beyond him; and even if he were to tell the boy the truth, there would be one certain result: it would mean that he would never see Simon again. Even now, he always felt uncomfortable with Nourganian – Nourganian knew; how much worse such knowledge on Simon's part would be.

At the same time, some sort of enlightening scene was necessary. If only he could tell the boy – but he was not sure what he wanted to tell him. Would he tell him how sorry he was for neglecting him for twenty-seven years? Or would he tell him that he was very fond of him? The truth was that he was more frightened of him than fond of him. The nearest thing to the truth that he could say was that he was guilty; that he had done him wrong and that, somehow or other, he wanted to atone for it.

This was certainly true; he felt he wanted some sort of object for his affections, but the trouble was that he had found it already in John Salvatori. He was equally sure that this was the wrong choice, but what could he do about that now?

'I was thinking about Christmas,' he said, interrupting the silence. 'I think it would be pleasant to invite Simon to luncheon here on the day itself. And I suppose you'd like to have a turkey, wouldn't you? Are you sure you won't have another pastelle?'

'No, thank you. But turkey would be wonderful.'

'I'd better tell the housekeeper at once,' said Alfred. 'She always likes to have plenty of notice, so she can give the thing a good week underground, you know, to make it tender.'

'Oh good,' said Salvatori, feeling his enthusiasm for Christmas fast evaporating. 'As soon as Christmas is over, we can start demolishing the old Cathedral.'

'So soon?'

'Yes. There are ten working days to go, and the concrete shell will be finished by then. It may even be finished before then. It is amazing what progress they have made.'

'I am looking forward to it,' said the Bishop, wondering whether things might not come to a head before Christmas were over.

13

THE WHOLE IDEA of things coming to a head, and the knowledge of how dangerous that would be, made Alfred restless after lunch. He could not very well go up to Seth's house and demand to see Simon, even though he thought the case was becoming urgent. He tried to convince himself that this was needless panic, but reassurance did not come. It came only when he had written his son a note, inviting him to call that evening. He left the note on the hall table, with instructions to his housekeeper to deliver it while she was in the town seeing to the death and burial of a turkey for Christmas.

The young man would certainly come. Respect for the clergy would ensure that. Alfred hoped that respect for the clergy would also guarantee certain other things too; that somehow or other he would be able to persuade the boy to abandon this absurd idea of being in love with Mr Seth's daughter. However, she wasn't his daughter, according to Salvatori; which meant that she had to be someone else's daughter. Perhaps that was the way to make her unsuitability clear to Simon. But, as it was her connexion with Seth that Alfred disapproved of, and that alone, making out that she was someone else's daughter might seem slightly incoherent. It was far better, perhaps, to leave the girl out of it entirely, and try and ram home how unsuitable the match was from Simon's point of view.

His filing cabinet contained records of all the financial trans-actions he had ever made. It was all there under lock and key and he had never thrown anything away. Somewhere among all that yellowing paper was some letter or some written evidence that testified to the money he had paid Simon's mother. All his files were dated, and he only had to find the one for the relevant year,

and see what he could discover. There was bound to be something relating to the buying of the fent-shop in Port of Spain; he
had bought the shop for her himself. If it ever became necessary
to prove to Simon who he was, this was the way.

He unlocked the filing cabinet and took out the file that had
reposed in tranquillity for twenty-seven years. Sure enough he
did find a letter that contained instructions to an agent about the
purchase of a shop in the name of Maria Scott. He saw his own
faded signature at the bottom. The rest of the file contained
lawyers' letters about the estate of his brother Hugo, who had
died in that year. He looked at them with a moment's idle
curiosity. Then he took the letter that might be useful in the
future and put it away in his desk drawer.

The possibility that the truth might emerge was very disturbing. Honesty was clearly not the best policy; he had known that
for years. The effects of honesty would almost certainly be dev-
astating. It was honesty that had got him sent to San Fernando.
And yet he had to stop this boy throwing himself away so
stupidly; but the best he could do was to try to probe, to test the
water, in order to find out how far he could venture in safety.
There was an element of risk.

He went out onto the verandah. Salvatori was nowhere to be
seen. Perhaps his Vicar-General had sensed that he wanted to be
alone; except he didn't want to be alone at all. He felt as he
looked down at San Fernando below him that he was standing on
the edge of a precipice and there was a terrible temptation to
throw himself over the edge. Very few people would be sorry; in
fact if the people around him had had more sense and more
sensitivity, wouldn't they have realised all along what was the
matter with him? If the Papal Nuncio who had made him a
Bishop had had an ounce of insight, wouldn't he not have made
him a Bishop? And even before that, wasn't there anyone who
could have seen the danger he ran with Maria Scott and pulled
him back from the edge? Had there never been anyone who had
bothered to look into his soul and understand it? There had been
no one; but the sadness was all the more bitter because it had

139

been his own fault. He had kept people at bay right from the start. He had wanted to do it all on his own, without any help from anyone, and when he had failed, how could he expect to find anyone who would comfort him?

As a matter of fact he had rather spurned Nourganian, a good kind man who would have loved to help him. But he didn't want to be helped. He wanted to be left alone, and was left alone, and yet still longed for human comfort. The desire was always there, but it was a desire he knew he would never fulfil as long as his pride held him back. But perhaps one day, in a moment such as this one, the misery of solitude would break even his pride and he would tell someone the whole story. This was a terrible danger. What if he were to tell Salvatori, Salvatori who was always so sympathetic?

It would be worse than suicide. John Salvatori would never look at him again without thinking that this was the high and mighty Bishop who had made love to one of his mother's servants. The most awful things happened to priests who fell from grace; everything else could be forgiven: alcoholism and financial mismanagement, gambling and breaking the speed-limit. But lust and illegitimate offspring were an enduring reproach. He could never tell anyone; and yet, might he have to tell Simon in order to stop him marrying Seth's daughter?

Towards evening, Simon came. They met on the verandah and, much to the Bishop's relief, Father Salvatori still seemed to be out of the house.

'How kind of you to come and see me,' said Alfred, wishing he did not sound so formal. 'I did call at your house this morning, but you were out. And I called at Da Silva as well, but you weren't there either.'

'I was at Mr Seth's,' said Simon.

'As far as I know,' said Alfred, 'I have never met Mr Seth. What is he like?'

Alfred sensed that this direct question was rather worrying; it was the sort of question that was not asked. Mr Seth was a sort of public secret: everyone knew about him, but no one ever discussed him, even though they knew that everyone knew. He was a subject that was talked around but never directly addressed. Some might hold him to be a good thing and others a bad one; but no one really had asked up to now what he was like.

Simon paused and thought about the question of Mr Seth. He would be honest and tell the truth; the truth, he had come to realise was always the simpler version, and the easier to express.

'Mr Seth is a black man,' he said. 'He has only got one eye. His empty eye-socket is all scarred and hideous, and I have been told that he was mutilated in a fight by someone called Tony Singh.'

'My father knew Tony Singh when he was in the Colonial Police,' said Alfred. 'Doesn't Seth wear an eye-patch?'

'Oh no. His disfigurement is a sort of trophy.'

'I see. Rather like a gladiator, then, his scars make him famous for toughness. I am beginning to get a picture of him. But go on.'

'I think that Seth is very rich indeed. He has a huge house and a swimming-pool and the whole place is like a fortress. All the windows have shutters and there's a high wall around the place. He has two bodyguards, I suppose you would call them, and at least two maids.'

'And are they the only people there?'

'No, there is this young girl,' said Simon, with an effort, for he felt now that it was important he should tell the Bishop, Christ's representative, everything. 'She is about twenty-five, I think. I don't know much about her, or how she ties in with the others. He says that she isn't his daughter.'

'Could she be attached to one of the bodyguards?' asked Alfred.

'Oh no,' said Simon at once. 'They're both such awful men. She isn't that sort of girl. At least, I don't think so. They are the worst type of thugs, and they look like it too. I can't picture her having anything to do with either of them.'

'Except she does live in the same house with them, doesn't she?' said Alfred. 'That means she must have a lot to do with them. She must see them every day and pass at least some of her time in their company. You may think it strange, my son, that I am asking all these questions ...'

'Not at all, Father,' said Simon, politely, using the less formal mode of address that he had tended to use with Nourganian. 'I know why you are asking. It is because Mr Seth is paying for the new Cathedral, and naturally you want to know something about him.'

'That is something I am concerned about,' said Alfred. 'It wouldn't do, to put it mildly, to build a Cathedral with dirty money. But if that is all, I would ask Father Salvatori, wouldn't I? But I am more concerned about you, my son. You see, before he went away, Mr Barratt came up here and told me certain things about Seth that he couldn't substantiate. I called up the Chief of Police and he told me another story entirely. And then Father Salvatori comes on the scene and tells me more or less the same thing the Chief told me: that Mr Seth is a very honest man. But they may be wrong; and if they are wrong, you are in danger of being led astray. So I must ask you, my son: is Mr Seth honest?'

'No, Father, he is not,' said Simon.

The words had come out straight away before he had had time to think. This was the bare unrehearsed truth. Suddenly, after a great deal of beating around the bush, they had arrived at it almost by accident.

'I feared as much,' said Alfred, seeing that this made things even more complicated than they had been before. 'Of course, there won't be a shred of evidence against the man ...'

'He is a thief,' said Simon. 'He is defrauding Da Silva; he hasn't paid us for the cement and sand he has ordered, or any of the building materials. The whole Cathedral is being financed by fraud. And he told me himself that one of his bodyguards is a murderer.'

What on earth had John Salvatori done, Alfred asked himself. 'We must try to be practical over this,' he said at last. 'Clearly, you can't allow yourself to co-operate with something that is a sin and a crime. You will have to resign your job.'

'And never go near Seth again?'

142

'Absolutely.'

Simon thought about what that would mean; the prospect of an absolute separation struck him as terrible indeed. 'It is impossible,' he said.

'It is quite possible,' answered the Bishop. 'And in the long run it will be far easier. What future is there here for you, with Seth bleeding Da Silva dry? I am sure Da Silva wouldn't mind shutting the place down. You could go back to Port of Spain.'

There was a clear logic to all this, but there was something in Simon's mind that resisted logic. 'I can't just leave the girl,' he said at last. 'And if they are as bad as you say they are, and I am sure they are that wicked, all the more reason not to leave her behind with them. I have to let her know that I can help her.'

'Help her? Has she asked you to rescue her?'

'No, but I feel – the fact is that I love her,' said Simon. He was used to confiding to the clergy and this was an easy declaration to make. He also felt that the word 'love' had the properties of a magic wand, and that when used, it somehow justified anything.

'Love, love, love,' said the Bishop with intense feeling. 'I know all about love. You are the victim of a terrible illusion. It isn't love that you feel; it is just that you are a good Catholic and you want to use this word to disguise what it really is. It is desire. The truth is that there is no one on God's earth, either among the children of darkness or the children of light, who hasn't felt the pangs of lust, and I mean a lust, a desire, a whatever you want to call it, directed at a specific person. We are so good at lying to ourselves, and trying to convince ourselves that we are somehow immune to this awful desire to possess another person, but no one is: not even the Pope himself.'

He had not spoken so vehemently about anything for twenty years, and he walked to the other end of the verandah in order to try and recover his usual sangfroid. But it was true – he had only told his son what he himself had learned some twenty-seven years ago.

Simon was left thinking about the girl; he could not raise

himself to abstract thoughts. He was too taken with the physical proximity that he had experienced that very afternoon. The girl had come to him by the pool-side. She had been accommodating, yet silent; welcoming yet withdrawn. Neither of them had spoken, and the intensity that might have been dissipated in words had been concentrated in their first kiss. He knew he was in love: he felt an aching lassitude over his whole body. And yet there were so many dangers involved. Perhaps she was, after all, being told to do this by Seth. Perhaps he was being set up by the old man. It might be some sort of elaborate trap. But he wanted her all the same: he had the desire to possess her. The Bishop was right: he knew nothing about her, but that didn't matter any more; all that mattered was that he should possess her, that he should own her. She was the object of his desires, nothing more.

'You have got to remember,' said Alfred, returning to the conversation with more aggressiveness than he wished. 'You can have nothing to do with these people. You are not like them, my son.'

'How on earth am I different, Father?' asked Simon.

'You're educated; you've been to a good school; you could have gone to university. You are not one of them. You can't have anything to do with thieves and murderers.'

'But I am one of them. The people who run Da Silva wouldn't be able to tell the difference between me and Seth. We're all blacks to them.'

'No, no, no,' said Alfred in anguish. 'I told you; you are one of the children of light and not one of the children of darkness.'

'I don't quite know the difference,' said Simon. 'I don't think I am anyone at all. I don't even know who my father was. I am an outcast like Seth. And being a good honest clerk in Da Silva for eight years hasn't got me very far.'

'Don't you know who your father was?' asked Alfred, feeling the weight of the secret within him.

'Not at all. And I am glad I don't know.'

'Why are you glad?'

'There are lots of reasons. My mother never told me, and she must have had her reasons. I think some white man raped her perhaps. She always had the look of a woman who was burdened by some awful knowledge, and maybe that was what gave her the illness that caused her death. It was cancer, you know. And besides, if my father had wanted to find me, there was nothing to stop him, was there? The reason he didn't find me was that he didn't care about us. The very best one could hope for was to find out that he had died ages ago; that would excuse his inexcusable absence.'

'But the Archbishop was kind to you, wasn't he?' asked Alfred hesitantly.

'Yes,' said Simon, lightening at the thought of the beloved Nourganian. 'He loves me like a son.'

There was something so simple and uncomplicated in this statement that it opened to Alfred a picture of what such a tranquil affection might be. At the same time it cut him to the quick to think that Nourganian had succeeded where he had failed.

'What would Archbishop Alphonsus think of Seth?' he asked.

At once Alfred saw that he had made more impression with this one question than with all he had said in the last twenty minutes. Simon was mute, and looked for a moment as though he might suddenly burst into tears. Clearly, Nourganian's love was able to do far more than any amount of Palmer-Ross logic. Alfred marvelled, for he had again caught a sudden glimpse into the true nature of love.

'I would hate to upset the Archbishop in any way,' said Simon at last. 'But how can I simply walk away from – all this?'

Simon looked at him as he spoke, and Alfred saw that he was telling the truth in all its bareness. In the young man's eyes he could see a reflection of his own self, as he had been twenty-seven years ago. He had never thought until now that Simon looked like him: but the resemblance was not just physical, the type that is discerned in a gesture or an expression of the face. He did, strangely enough, notice a resemblance to his elder brother, Hugo, at that moment in the expression in the eyes. But, more

145

than that, he recognised an emotion that he himself had experienced himself at more ór less the same age. Simon was in that unenviable position of being about to do something wrong in the full knowledge of its wrongness, and at the same time being unable to tear himself away from it, and yet unable quite to deceive himself into thinking that the wrong was right. Perhaps this predicament was hereditary, for that was exactly the feeling that Alfred himself had experienced the last time he had gone to Maria Scott, the time his son was conceived.

'I must see her at least one more time,' he said.

'Something terrible will happen to you,' said Alfred gloomily. Then he remembered that the boy had been born of his mistake, and added: 'But good can come out of evil.'

'I know something terrible will happen to me,' said Simon, 'But it's no good my trying to frighten myself. It has no effect.'

'Sometimes they say we have to make mistakes so that we can learn from them,' said Alfred. 'That is how the liberals interpret Saint Augustine, when he says even sin can be for the glory of God when properly repented of. I am not sure if I can quite swallow it, though.'

Simon got up to go.

'Don't go yet,' said Alfred. 'I'd quite forgotten why I asked you to come here. Father Salvatori and I would be so pleased if you would come here to have Christmas lunch with us.'

'Thank you, I would like to very much.'

'Good,' said Alfred weakly. He wished he had the courage to ask the young man what he thought exactly of Father Salvatori; but he dared not do it.

'Well, then,' he said after a pause. He made an awkward little gesture of benediction. 'God bless you, my son,' he said.

14

DURING THE WEEK that led up to Christmas, Alfred found that he was worrying about John Salvatori.

What was to be done about him?

This was not the usual trouble caused by the Archbishop's having recommended him, and the Bishop's not liking him. That sort of thing was common enough; Bishops were continually having unwanted priests passed off on them by wily superiors. That sort of problem could usually be dealt with in a variety of well-known ways. Unwanted priests could always, as a last resort, be given warm recommendations for the missions. But Alfred liked John; he didn't want to get rid of him; he liked him in the way a parent liked a spoilt child. He found himself unable to utter even an unkind or harsh word to him, or a syllable of reproof. He did not want to hurt his feelings or, more accurately, he didn't want to hurt his own feelings in the matter, as he enjoyed indulging him. He was an overfond father, and a bad one too. But this didn't diminish the fact that Mr Seth was not the ideal friend for the Vicar-General. This circumlocution disguised the unpleasant and unpalatable truth that Salvatori was corrupt, a priest who used the Church, a hedge-priest. This was the unavoidable conclusion that he had tried to avoid for too long. He was the sort of priest that Alfred, in his Anglo-Saxon way, thought of as typically Italian. But what could he say to him?

The days passed, and he kept a prudent silence instead of speaking. And if it were not bad enough that Salvatori was in cahoots with Seth, a man whose bodyguard was supposed to be a murderer, he forced himself to think how Salvatori had actually fostered the friendship between Seth and Simon Palmer, encouraging the young man to become the old criminal's protégé. When he thought of this, standing on his verandah, Alfred felt a wave of moral outrage, and resolved to do something about it. He would speak to Salvatori at once, as soon as he returned; he resolved this at least once a day, and yet just as often, when he saw Salvatori's smiling face, he put the confrontation off for the morrow.

The days passed, and Salvatori, like Sheherazade, lived another day. Other excuses arose: one could hardly have a show-down with the Vicar-General, and wreck one's domestic tranquillity, so close to Christmas. It was the season of goodwill, after all. He would face the problem in the new year.

But these thoughts oppressed Alfred only when Salvatori was absent, when he was in the town supervising his building-site; Salvatori's presence could drive away any melancholy thoughts. For the first time in years, for the first time in his life perhaps, Alfred found himself enjoying someone's company, and even coming to rely on it. The prospect of John being taken away from him was frightening, for what would he do without him? How had he ever managed to fill the barren hours and years before his arrival? How difficult it would now be if he were forced to live on his own again; he could not go back to his solitary life, for he had seen how different life could be. He no longer wanted to be alone all the time. In the past he had continually craved solitude. Even – no, particularly – the experience of physical love had driven him to want to be alone with himself, without others. He had been fond of his relations once; dear they might have been, but he had never wanted them particularly near him, but now time hung heavy on his hands when he was alone. When John was not there, he found that he could not settle to anything. He had tried to write a new article for the *Tablet* – a review of a biography of Heidegger – which dwelled on the fact that private worlds were formed by public ones, but when he tried to think of Heidegger he found his mind filling with John. Where was he? What was he doing? And was he with Simon, or was he at Seth's? This was a frequent question during that week, and the answer he feared was yes in both cases. He wished it was not so. Time and again he stood on his verandah and looked at the town and regretted his imprisoning isolation. San Fernando could not be so dull a place if it could so often draw John Salvatori there. And he realised that he was a fool and that he could not help it.

This feeling of his, though it shared many of the symptoms of human love, was, he knew, nothing of the sort. He did not love Salvatori; he found him necessary for his amusement. He did not will his highest good, but merely found him useful, in fact, more than useful, he found him absolutely necessary. That was what was so foolish about the whole thing. He had allowed himself to be beguiled.

As the days passed the view had changed. The familiar brown shape of the wooden Cathedral had been progressively obscured by rising concrete walls. A few days before Christmas Eve itself the new roof seemed to have appeared. It was quite astounding how fast you could build with concrete. It was not at all like laying bricks, a tedious and slow one at a time process. Concrete buildings seemed to involve huge panels and moulded shapes that were heaved into place by a large crane, which bore the one word SETH on it, written in huge letters. Concrete buildings were built in the same manner a child built with Lego. They were fitted together hurriedly. The swiftness of the procedure, the speed with which this new construction had appeared, gave Alfred a stab of anxiety. It had gone up without his having a chance to examine at close quarters what was being built. If he were to go down now and raise objections at the eleventh hour, what good would it do? He had spent too long moping on his verandah. It was better to wait until the thing was finished, and hope for the best.

But the anxiety he felt was destined to be disturbed that very night by Salvatori himself.

'Midnight Mass will be the first Mass in the new building,' he said casually that night. 'The shell is ready, and there's no reason why we shouldn't start the demolition of the old building tomorrow; it should be very quick.'

'That is ...' said Alfred, not quite able to get out the word 'wonderful'. 'Isn't that a little precipitate?' he asked instead.

'It really is time we brought it down,' said Salvatori soothingly. 'And it really does seem to me that Midnight Mass is the best time for the transformation. It is the feast of the new birth and all that, after all. And the people are so looking forward to it. They've made heaps of preparations. Of course, there will be no electric light as yet, but we can use candles, and they have gone to such lengths with the music.'

'Music?' asked Alfred fearfully.

'Oh yes, they think that the Bishop's Mass should be liturgically exciting. They're quite right, of course, aren't they? Vatican Two and all that.'

'Perhaps it might be better if you said the Midnight Mass,' said Alfred.

'Oh, I couldn't,' he protested. 'They expect you to do it; they're very keen on the idea of Bishops.'

'Are they? I suppose they must be, and if they seem to expect it, I shall have to do my best to oblige them. I see so little of them, I suppose I hardly have the right to complain. But I wonder about Bishops: they seemed to like the old Vicar-General far more than they ever liked me.'

'We shall see,' said Salvatori. 'All the altar boys have been practising for days.'

'And the building itself ...'

'Will look magnificent,' he was assured.

*

Christmas was approaching; even Simon felt it. It could not have come at a worse time. The last Christmas he had spent in Port of Spain; although only a year had passed, it seemed a lifetime away. That Christmas, his mother having recently died, the Archbishop had invited him to lunch. He knew that the Archbishop was still

150

thinking of him, for Nourganian had rung him up and suggested that he come up to Port of Spain for a few days, while Da Silva was shut. But he had other plans; fortunately he was able to tell the Archbishop that Monsignor Palmer-Ross had invited him to Christmas lunch and that he could not come to Port of Spain. It was not a lie, but it gave him the same feeling of guilt that a lie would have done. He wanted to stay in San Fernando, for Seth had told him that Burke and Payne were going to Tobago together over Christmas to visit their aged mother, and that he, Simon, would have to keep him company in their absence. He had sensed something was afoot; and he had guessed that Seth was growing tired of Burke.

A little later Seth had been even more direct. He was thinking of getting rid of Burke, he said. Burke was becoming something of a liability to him. How he would get rid of him he did not as yet know, he maintained, but the trip that he was to take to Tobago was something to do with it.

'Perhaps,' mused Seth quietly, 'perhaps the police could deal with Burke. Not when he is here, but when he is in Tobago. The Chief might arrange it.'

'What does that mean?' asked Simon.

'The Chief could arrest him for some past misdeed,' said Seth. 'But there's no saying what Burke might do if he thinks I have betrayed him. He thinks I ought to be grateful to him. And then there is always Payne.'

'Will the police arrest him as well?'

'Payne is not guilty of much,' said Seth. 'He was always Burke's shadow. I was thinking that, as Payne always was jealous of Burke, he might tip him overboard on the ferry to Tobago, so the sharks would get him.'

'But he is his brother.'

'There is that disadvantage,' said Seth. 'I don't think Payne would do anything directly ...'

And then the subject was dropped. But it did not go away. Burke was clearly falling out of favour. Mr Seth was hankering after legality. And the girl, Pattie, wanted Burke out of the way. Simon knew it: she would not speak to him when Burke was in the house. But when Burke went away, she promised she would be less reserved. She too feared Burke. And so did Simon. There was something animal-like about the man. That he had committed murder was almost of academic interest to Simon; that he frightened Pattie was enough to make him hate him.

He had discovered her name. It had been volunteered readily enough the second time they had been alone together. Once Burke was gone the rest would follow. He knew that now; her actions no less than her words told him as much. And though he would go to Mass on Christmas night with all the best intentions in the world, he knew how useless they would be.

*

'It will be magnificent,' John Salvatori had said.

Magnificent was not the word that Alfred used to himself when, on Christmas Eve, he walked down to view the ruins in the hot afternoon. The old Cathedral had been pulled down – only its floor and its benches remained. The old altar stood under its concrete vault, orphaned. Everywhere there was concrete: a concrete nave and concrete aisles, with concrete pillars dividing them. The windows, high above and as yet unglazed, let the harsh inhospitable sunlight in, to fall on the rough grey surfaces. It was not at all like his memories of the Basilica of John and Paul.

'I told you it would be magnificent,' said John from behind him. 'I mean, the space, the light.'

'Of course, it is not finished yet,' said Alfred, not turning round.

'We have to think about the windows,' conceded John. 'And we will have to get a new altar. But really it is more or less finished in its essence.'

'And the walls?'

'Are a triumph,' said John. 'They are just like the ancient catacombs, rough and unhewn.'

'I see. I hadn't realised that you admired concrete so much.'

152

'It's the material of the future,' said John. 'If they were building St Peter's today, this is what it would look like.'

'Would it?' said Alfred. He had always disliked Saint Peter's and found it vulgar, Italianate and more like a film-set than a church. But now he felt a certain sympathy for the baroque. Concrete was the material of the future: he therefore was a bishop of the past.

Leaving the happy Vicar-General, he made his weary way up the hill. Something horrible had happened. In a few hours, that very night, he had to celebrate Mass in a building that resembled an aircraft hangar. It was his own fault. He had given John Salvatori *carte blanche*, and this was how he had used it. He blamed his own terrible judgment. He had misjudged Salvatori: he had trusted the man's taste and now found out that he had none. It was almost more than he could bear. Letting the Cathedral be demolished and having a jerry-built monstrosity put up in its place was bad enough – but far worse was the painful realisation that he was no judge of people. He had been foolish and had no one to blame but himself. How could he have allowed himself to be so totally taken in by a charlatan, an Italian mountebank like Salvatori? All his old prejudices against Italians came back to him as he sweated up the hill; they were very charming, but they simply couldn't be trusted. They would take the most terrible advantage of you, and then have the barefaced cheek to expect you to forgive them, as if it were their right. They were like children, easily offended, quick to anger, and equally quick to affection. They were infuriating in every way. Why hadn't he remembered that when he had first come across Salvatori? The man was an Italian, after all.

He was getting angry. There was nothing quite like religion for bringing out the worst in people. Quite charming people, reasonable in all else, were stubborn enough to become heretics, and in happier times there had been others, equally intolerant, who had been only too keen to burn them at the stake. Of course, a heretic could always repent and get off, but so few actually had: people would rather face the flames than compromise on such questions as the existence of multiple worlds. Building up the Church was all very well, but the whole idea of Church seemed to incite some people to frenzies of destruction. If they weren't burning each other, they were burning altars and rood screens. Henry VIII, that great lover of the arts, hadn't been able to keep his hands off the monasteries. They had made charming ruins, but that wasn't the point at all. The point was that deep in human nature was a spirit of turbulence, a desire to put God into the place where man thought He ought to be, a desire that wanted to level anything that was built for His glory. It was a sort of universal illness, this vandalism, this awful pride that put the human being at the centre of everything, banishing the Creator as if to the icy limits of the solar system. Everything had to revolve around them, these uncontrollable egos, of which John Salvatori was but the latest example. You picked and chose what suited you; it was supermarket religion, to be practised, if at all, in churches built to look like supermarkets. It depressed Alfred. God would survive it, but would *he*?

He took his sense of betrayal with him into the house. He hadn't thought that John would do this to him. But John, he reflected, was too unthinking to notice his distress or even to understand why he should mind his Cathedral being pulled down. And then John might have some excuse: for he had not tried to stop him. He hadn't thought he would need to.

Much as he would have liked to pretend to be ill in order to escape the coming ordeal, he knew he had to go through with the Midnight Mass. There was no escaping it, and at midnight he was there, as he had been the year before.

He was wearing his episcopal best, all scarlet and black, and he had carefully typed out his sermon some weeks before, a nice little meditation on the words 'Today is born to you a Saviour, who is Christ the Lord'. The sermon was one he had used, with modifications, many years before. It centred on the use of the word 'today', and how every Christmas night was the actualisation of that eternal today, the day of Christ's birth. Salvatori, ever-present, guided him through the first part of the Mass.

154

When it came to the sermon, he sat alone at the front of the altar as Bishops did, and read his script. This in itself presented some difficulty as there was only candle-light to read by. He did not look at the congregation as he read, but pondered what he was saying: it was as if he were giving a radio broadcast to an unseen and unseeing audience, as if he were some actor reading lines in which he did not believe.

When it came to the Eucharistic prayer, he stood at the altar marooned in darkness. The congregation had held lighted candles for the first hour of the service, but one by one these had gone out, leaving a solitary pool of watery light on the altar alone, provided by the six large candles there. (Among the last to put out his candle had been a black man who had stood out from the rest of the congregation, by reason of his facial disfigurement, which, illuminated by a guttering taper, had been as hideous as a voodoo mask.)

The choir, if they deserved to be designated such, had just finished their rendition of the Calypso version of the Sanctus. In the darkness and the silence that succeeded, Alfred hesitated: he felt as if he was the last priest on earth, as if he were celebrating Mass not to mark the Birth of the Saviour, but for the disfigured survivors of a nuclear catastrophe. Thus would Christianity end, if it ever came to that, amidst darkness, disfigurement and concrete. Concrete was sinister; and in concrete bunkers people fled to die. But next to him he sensed John Salvatori, adjusting the Missal in the mistaken belief that he could not see it properly. A cough escaped from the unseen congregation.

'We come to you, Father, with praise and thanksgiving,' whispered Salvatori, prompting him.

'We come to you, Father,' intoned Alfred, 'with praise and thanksgiving.'

In his heart he felt very different. But still the familiar words carried him onwards.

'Grant us your peace in this life,' he was now saying. 'Save us from final damnation and count us among those you have chosen.'

Then came the words of consecration. He stopped. He tried to compose himself for the most important words of the Mass, the words that would constitute the Christian miracle. He gazed ahead into the darkness. Everyone was kneeling down, heads bowed in prayer. Then a strange thing happened. Someone in the congregation struck a match and relit a candle. He immediately saw that it was the man with the devil's mask of a face. Next to him, illuminated by the same candle, and in fact holding it for him, acting as the devil's torch-bearer was his son. He saw Simon's pleasant face illuminated. Then the candle flickered and went out, and all was darkness once more.

Paralysis gripped his throat. He could not say the words. Even if he were to say them, they would have no meaning. For in that fateful pause, he now realised, faith had deserted him. The words up to now had carried him through – for twenty years he had relied on words – but now even the forms of things had deserted him. To consecrate the Body and Blood of Christ was beyond him entirely. Instead, all he saw was the blackness in front of him, the horrible emptiness of it all.

'Go on,' said Salvatori calmly, his finger actually on the words on the printed page.

He had no need for the helpful finger. The words were clear enough, printed in huge capitals: THIS IS MY BODY. THIS IS THE CUP OF MY BLOOD. The words were clear enough.

'Go on,' he heard Salvatori say, a little less calmly.

'You say it,' said Alfred. 'You are a priest.'

'I'll say the words but you say them with me,' he said to the Bishop.

Salvatori uttered the words firmly and loudly, and did so using a passable imitation of Alfred's way of speaking. Disaster, thought the Vicar-General, had been averted; for, with this hurdle out of the way, the Bishop suddenly continued the Mass. He did so with no animation, as if he were reading out something mundane and banal; then, when it was finally over, they retired to the soon-to-be-demolished wooden sacristy. The congregation, an exceptionally large one, stood and sang.

'Is something the matter?' asked Salvatori, when the altar boys were out of the way. There was a slight edge of annoyance to his voice.

'Yes,' said Alfred. 'Something is, as you put it, the matter.' He stood by the vestment press as he said this, his hands motionless, resting on the dull wooden surface. 'I have been a priest for thirty years. I have said Mass every day for thirty years. I must have said Mass over ten thousand times. It was familiar to me. It was what I had been anointed to do. I used to handle the Body of Christ with familiarity, but not with contempt. I thought I was one of the chosen ones.'

'What do you mean?' asked Salvatori quietly.

'I haven't been a Bishop at all,' said Alfred. 'Not these twenty years. I have been a waste of time.'

'You're feeling tired, that's all,' said Salvatori. 'It is almost two in the morning. Perhaps we had better –'

'No. I don't feel tired at all, and I am not hysterical or anything like that,' said Alfred calmly. 'You haven't understood what I have been saying. There was nothing there. I looked out from the altar and I stared into emptiness. I saw that it was all empty.'

'It was dark.'

'And then I knew. God wasn't there, hadn't been there. God is always greater. Your Cathedral, John, can't contain God. All this is empty. The real God is beyond me entirely. I looked out and I saw it all.'

'You mean,' said Salvatori cautiously, 'You have had a vision?'

'Yes, a vision.'

'Like at Lourdes?' he asked, his mind immediately picturing coachloads of pilgrims, souvenir shops and a tourist boom.

'Lourdes is what people would expect,' said Alfred. 'Something that even unbelievers can understand, something that can be marketed and turned to profit. But God isn't like that. The God you expect to live in this Cathedral may be like that, but you only see what you want to see. The reality is far beyond. You prefer the picture-postcards, John, to the real thing.'

157

'I don't understand,' said John. 'Do you mean to tell me that you've seen God?'

'I think I may have seen the devil. I saw Mr Seth and my son, and I realised that I have − I suppose you would understand me if I said that I had ruined my life?'

'But you haven't got a son,' said Salvatori. 'You must be having delusions. Look, you really must come back with me, as soon as all the people have cleared off. We can go up to the house. You are obviously not yourself.'

'I am now completely myself. I have never felt as though I were myself up to this moment,' said Alfred. Then he added: 'You thought Simon was Nourganian's.'

'Oh God,' said Salvatori, and sat down rather suddenly. His blond face had gone suddenly paler.

'You thought I was a Bishop,' said Alfred. 'But when I saw them together, something changed. I realised that the most important thing of all is loving those who are close to us and not thinking about ourselves, and that for all these years I have been imprisoned by my own stupid self.' He said this without bitterness.

'For God's sake, shut up,' hissed Salvatori, now sufficiently recovered to be able to feel the onset of panic. 'Someone might hear you. I had better clear the church and lock it up, and then when the coast is clear I will walk up with you. And I'd better keep him away.'

Salvatori took off his vestments and went out into the new Cathedral again. It was cold, dark and empty. Most of the people had gone home; only a few of them seemed to be hanging around outside in the warm December night.

'I want to wish the Monsignor a Happy Christmas,' he heard a voice say.

It was Simon.

'He's awfully tired,' said Salvatori.

'Oh well, I'll see him tomorrow anyway. What time is lunch? At noon?'

'Yes,' said Salvatori. 'I'll see you then.'

Salvatori disappeared into the concrete hulk. Seth, who had

stood by in the shadows, now approached. Simon, put out by the priest's off-hand and hurried manner, did not notice him at first.

'Drive me home,' said Seth. 'Pattie is waiting up for me with some drinks; and none of the other boys are here to drive me home.'

He put some car-keys into his hands, which shone and jangled in the darkness.

*

Later, when the sound of a car had finally died away, when all was silent and calm, Salvatori led the Bishop out of the Cathedral, his prisoner, almost, and walked with him up the hill. They went in silence; and in silence Alfred went straight to bed. Salvatori saw him do so, went into the sitting-room, wished he could drink some whisky, and settled down with a rum instead.

Sleep was clearly impossible. It was now half-past-two in the morning. Archbishop Nourganian, he knew, always got up at about four-thirty; but perhaps at Christmas his habits would be different. He could hardly dare phone until six at the earliest; yet he could hardly dare wait either. It was an emergency, after all: the Bishop had clearly had a breakdown. John did not quite know what had happened to him, but the general term 'breakdown' was a useful one. That was the word he would use on the phone. Perhaps he should call at once and wake up Nourganian. But that might be counter-productive. It wouldn't do to annoy the old man; and it wouldn't do to phone without having everything properly worked out in his mind. He had to know what to say.

He tried to think clearly. He sipped his rum. This was what was called a scandal. The Bishop had admitted that he was the father of a young man. Simon was in his mid-twenties, he knew, but scandals kept their freshness. If anyone were to find out – and he had a vision of newspaper headlines – then that would be terrible. Nourganian would go to any lengths to prevent that. And if Alfred Palmer-Ross were to behave as he had behaved tonight, and he might very well do that sort of thing again, everyone

159

would know it before long. Resignation was the only thing, once the guilty secret was out. And the secret was out; he, John Salvatori, knew it. This too presented problems. If it were true, Palmer-Ross would hardly want to keep him on. How could he live in the same house with a man who knew he was the father of the clerk at Da Silva, and who knew that the Bishop had been to bed with a black woman, or perhaps even more than one? Palmer-Ross had to resign; the alternative – Salvatori's own departure to save the Bishop's embarrassment – was unthinkable.

Palmer-Ross would resign. He could force it; he could insist that the Bishop went, for the good of the Church of course. But the chief beneficiary would be himself, John Salvatori, now future Bishop of San Fernando. His foot was almost now on the bottom of the episcopal ladder – for in a sudden change, who were they likely to appoint other than the man on the job already? A young energetic bishop – just the solution for a diocese that had been neglected too long.

He would phone Nourganian at six that morning. He had to seize the moment. He knew his personal number, the one of the phone by his bedside. He would do it. And with this resolution he went up to bed.

As he tried to sleep, he wondered how on earth Alfred Palmer-Ross had ever come to love Mrs Palmer, Simon's mother. He remembered her fairly well. She had been an unremarkable woman. To think that the foolish man was ruining himself for love of her, so long after the event and even after she was dead. And with that he fell asleep.

*

He was awake again and ringing up Port of Spain at six.

'Yes,' said Nourganian, at the other end of the line.

'John Salvatori here. I am afraid that something has gone wrong with the Bishop. He was unable to say the words of consecration at the Mass last night. He told me that he was the father of Simon Palmer.'

160

'I see,' said the Archbishop, unperturbed, as if this was what he was expecting, even hoping, to hear.

'But is it true? About Palmer?'

'Yes, it is true.'

'I don't know what to do next,' said Salvatori. 'I don't think I can deal with this on my own.'

'In fact,' said Nourganian, 'I was thinking of coming down to San Fernando myself. It is strange you should call me. You see, I wanted to see Simon, and as he can't come here for Christmas I was thinking of coming down. Why don't you expect me some time today?'

This was better than he could have hoped for. He put down the phone. Of course, he had betrayed his master. He had hardly slept more than a few hours, but he felt excited, even euphoric. If Nourganian were to think that Palmer-Ross was disturbed in some way, or too grave a risk of causing public scandal, he might bundle him away somewhere that very night. The Kingdom would then pass to him. He would inherit it, and the mighty would be dispossessed.

As for the Bishop himself, he had little sympathy for him. He had slept with a black woman, fathered a child and then been foolish enough to let it prey on his mind. This was unforgivable weakness. He could not understand how Palmer-Ross could throw everything away so easily. Of course, it was Seth's doing: it was Seth who had done it somehow; he had seen Seth in the Cathedral with Simon, and it had driven him over the edge. 'You don't understand,' the Bishop had said to him the night before. There was something a little condemnatory in all this, he now suspected. He had not understood – what? Seth? That Seth was somehow evil? But he had only been kind to Seth to get the Cathedral built, and if he had arranged for Seth to use Simon, that had only been for the greater glory of God. Hadn't St Peter's been built by selling indulgences? Hadn't Our Lord hung around with tax collectors and prostitutes? And who was Palmer-Ross to be so moral when he had sinned so spectacularly himself? The sooner he went the better, thought John. But he had one little fear: namely, that Palmer-Ross should determine to stay on in order to stop him, the builder of the magnificent new Cathedral, being consecrated as his successor.

What if Palmer-Ross were to tell the truth about Seth? That thought gave him pause on the threshold of his triumph.

15

ALFRED AWOKE late and puzzled. He stared at the ceiling and wondered if he were still in San Fernando. He felt he ought to be elsewhere. There would be a poetic justice in waking up and finding himself on some desert island, or in a prison cell. He adjusted himself to consciousness and felt a terrible heaviness in all his limbs. The previous night had exhausted him. He was drained. It was as if all his internal organs had been removed and the cavities stuffed with sawdust. They did that to corpses sometimes. The blood in his veins felt like formaldehyde, cold and sluggish. It was as if he were dead: and he was dead. The previous night, before falling asleep, he had reviewed his life, watched it go by him, like some rather dull film that he had seen before and did not care to see again. This was the life that was now past, finished with, dead. Nothing was left. Even the episcopal anointing he had received from Pope Paul in the Vatican – it was as if that had never been, or had happened to someone else. He was an ex-Bishop now, just as he had become an ex-Palmer-Ross. He was now a man with no name lying there in his pyjamas, a man no one would care about any more, and as he remembered that, he had a feeling of liberation.

He had discovered something last night on the altar. He had seen something, but could not quite remember what it had been; it was like one of those vivid dreams that vanishes the moment one wakes. But it had been something important and something incommunicable. He remembered now how he had tried to explain it to Salvatori and failed to do so. That something that he had realised so suddenly was now beyond him, unreachable and remote. Would it ever come back? And if it did not come back to him, what would he do? He saw himself wandering the world in search of this unattainable vision. That would be hell: to see for a moment the glory of God and then to know that one was forever cut off from it. But he had not seen the glory of God. That belonged to the next life. In this life there were merely moments of intense knowledge, and last night he had been granted one of those.

He dragged his heavy body out of bed. As he steadied himself in front of the shaving mirror he realised something else. He had told Salvatori the secret. He ought to see Salvatori at once, to try and find out what he would do. The realisation that there was something to be done, something urgent, gave him the energy to wash and dress, to put on his pectoral cross and go downstairs.

The house was silent, as if it too had sensed the change that had taken place. It was as deserted as a ship, alone on the high seas. Alfred felt a blinding sense of panic creep up on him, and he half stumbled towards the kitchen, when he found every other room empty. There was the housekeeper, shocked to see him, for it was the first time he had been in the kitchen in years. He asked her where Father Salvatori had gone. To say Mass, of course, she replied, looking at him a little oddly. After all, it was Christmas Day. She suggested a cup of coffee. He took it from her, and then went into the hall, where the telephone was ringing.

It was the Archbishop.

'I thought I would join you for Christmas lunch,' Nourganian was saying at the other end. 'I don't eat very much, you know, so don't worry about the food. There is nothing to keep me here at present, and Simon told me he would be with you. I would like to see him. And John Salvatori has been on the phone asking me to come down.'

'Already?'

'Yes. I am afraid so. But I was hoping to come anyway.'

'I see,' said Alfred.

He rather absently put the receiver down, cutting off the Archbishop. He did indeed see. Salvatori had not wasted any time; he had moved in for the kill while his opportunity lasted. Everything was crumbling. He sat down in the sitting-room and contemplated his ruin. He had not said Mass, or his breviary, or made his meditation; he had fulfilled none of his mechanical duties. But that old life was gone. He sat on, paralysed: this was the sort of thing one heard whispered about. White men went into the jungle as missionaries or colonial administrators and were never seen again, unless by chance they were discovered, clad in rags, chattering incomprehensibly, by some compatriot chancing upon them years later. He himself had had an uncle in the Sierra Leone customs whom no one ever discussed. Presumably he had gone native or gone mad, or both. Something, as they said, snapped; that thin cord that held you to conventional behaviour and the habits of a lifetime. You stopped pretending; you stopped caring about people realising what you were really like. And people, the anonymous but tyrannous 'they', always reacted with horror. It even happened with elephants. To leave the herd meant permanent isolation.

John Salvatori came in, rosy-cheeked from celebrating the morning Mass of the Nativity. He had thought there was no one in the room; then he saw Alfred and stopped with a little start.

'Nourganian will be here for lunch,' said Alfred.

'Oh good.'

'He told me you had phoned him.'

'I did.'

'I see.'

'What do you see?' asked Salvatori, adopting the tone of a concerned optician.

'I see it all,' said Alfred.

'I still don't understand you,' said Salvatori.

'You have betrayed me,' said Alfred, without bitterness. It was as if he were stating a fact, a remote event, something that had happened on the other side of the world.

'I haven't betrayed you,' said Salvatori, wounded by the word.

'I suppose not,' conceded Alfred. 'Please don't think that I resent it. What I meant was, I thought you were more devoted to me than that. Except I never really thought that. I quite understand your motives. I have been a ludicrous Bishop. I have hardly

165

been near my diocese these twenty years. The vast majority of the Catholics here have never seen me. You have done well to take the opportunity, and I am sure you will be rewarded.'

'Do you really think so? Will you put in a word with the Archbishop?' asked Salvatori.

Alfred looked at him. The man could not disguise what he really wanted, after all. One could not blame Salvatori. His bland, vacuous face told the entire story. It was absurd to think that he had ever thought the man was anything other than he was. He was a placeman. It was his own stupidity that had seen him as anything else.

'I know what you want me to do,' said Alfred. 'You want me to go to Nourganian and say that I have decided to resign and that I want you to replace me, because you are such a fine young priest, and because there is no one better suited than the incumbent Vicar-General anyway. I could even add the fact that I would have resigned years ago if I had known that such an excellent successor were possible. Is that what you want me to say?'

'Only if you want to say it,' said John, guardedly, trying to control his breathing. He could almost feel the prize dangling before him. He wondered if this was some sort of elaborate trap. It was almost too much to believe, this thought that suddenly what he had wanted for so long was going to be handed to him on a plate.

'Be honest and tell me what you want me to say.'

'Yes. I want you to tell him you will resign and that you want me to be Bishop after you.'

'It will happen anyway,' said Alfred. 'I won't do any harm if I add my voice to the Papal Nuncio's. And I don't want to stay here anyway, if only you could realise that.'

But Salvatori was not listening. He was kneeling down in front of his patron, kissing his ring enthusiastically.

'You are a clever young person,' said Alfred. 'You know how to handle people. A lot of people will be happy about this. Nourganian will be pleased. I suppose Simon will be too.'

'And won't you be pleased as well?' asked Salvatori, relinquishing his hand, looking up into his face.

Alfred saw then what it meant to want to be loved, to want to be approved of.

'I'll be quite pleased,' he said.

Alfred smiled at the sheer audacity of Salvatori. He was beginning to forgive him his ambitions already. There was something extraordinary about a man who could do so much for so paltry a prize – for it was hardly worth selling one's soul to be Bishop of San Fernando – and still expect his victim to approve of him in the end. Such an attitude spoke of invincible Italian charm.

*

Simon had woken up. His first thought was that it was the morning of Christ's Nativity. His second thought was of himself and his strange position.

He could feel, without opening his eyes that he was in an unfamiliar bed and that he was unclothed. That much was certainly true. He could smell the peculiar smell, a not unpleasant smell, that spoke of intimacy: a mixture of cheap scent, sweat and unwashed clothing. Still without opening his eyes, he stretched out his hand, but instead of the warm reposeful body that he had expected, he felt only the hollow in the mattress where she had fallen asleep.

He opened his eyes. He was alone. The room was dark still, but there were no curtains; it was dark because it was about to rain. There was a distant rumble of thunder. The clock by the bedside told him that it was ten in the morning; it was a 24-hour clock, and there was no mistaking the time: this alleviated any incipient anxiety about having overslept and missed lunch with the Bishop. But, even so, there was something strange about being in this unfamiliar room. It was eerily silent too; there was no sound from outside, a sure sign that a sudden downpour was imminent. He could see through the net door into the familiar garden which was as still as a drawing.

There was no sign of Pattie. He was glad of it. She had disappointed him. He had experienced transports of delight with her, so it was not her fault. However, the complete experience that he had sought had eluded him. In the midst of all their exertions something had failed to happen. He had failed to love her. What should have happened was what he had always imagined happening: it should have marked the beginning of an indissoluble union. He should, even now, be holding her in his arms and swearing that no power on earth would ever separate them. Instead of that, he was glad that she wasn't there; he was glad to be alone. Sex had its moments of pleasure, but there was something so restful about being alone after it was over. Perhaps he should get up and slip out of the house, without her finding him lying in her bed. That would be the best thing to do. Then he could take his new-found delight in solitude with him down the hill. That was the trouble about being in love: as soon as you stepped back from the experience and saw it from outside, you realised how ridiculous you had been.

He heaved himself up into a sitting position. His clothes were still where he had left them, neatly folded on a chair. There had been something a little too planned about their going to bed together the night before. It had been a consummation that had occupied his mind for at least the previous week, but when the time for it had come – after Seth had left them alone – it had all been done with too much precision. They had gone to the bedroom and undressed very carefully without looking at each other, and then got into the double bed without a word. How foolish he was to have thought that he had actually loved her. He hadn't. She was a stranger to him, an expert stranger who had taken him over. The impersonal nature of the encounter was reflected in the room. There was nothing of her in it. It was like a man's room.

It was a man's room.

He noticed that there was an expensive-looking electric razor on the table next to the bed. He picked it up and flicked the switch: it made an aggressive whirring noise, very loud against

168

the background silence. He got up and began to examine the furniture. A drawer revealed male underwear. Another drawer was full of a woman's underwear. A wardrobe disclosed a collection of suits, shirts and trousers, never worn by Pattie. They were familiar; he had seen Burke wearing them. He had spent the night in Burke's bedroom. Pattie was Burke's wife, as the Bishop had surmised. Now that he was no longer besotted with her, he realised that this must indeed be so. Perhaps she would soon be Burke's widow, if Seth was going to get rid of Burke, as he had loosely said he would. Simon, standing naked in the middle of the room, realised that he was in some sort of ill-defined danger.

'Oh God,' he said, out loud.

He wondered if there was any danger at that very moment. He tried to reason. Burke and Payne were in Tobago; they would hardly arrive at ten in the morning on Christmas Day. But he only had Seth's word for it that they had gone there. Seth was surely telling the truth, though, for what would Seth gain if Burke came back to find that Seth had allowed him to sleep with his wife while he was away? And in his own bed too. Burke would kill Seth as soon as he had dealt with Simon himself, and Seth could hardly want that. Seth would only want something useful to himself.

A crack of thunder outside announced the beginning of the downpour. Simon went to the door and saw the rain rapidly become torrential. Then he stepped out into the warm water. The water cleansed him of the fear he had felt. Now he felt that he had been taken in indeed; Seth had planned all this; Seth had thought himself so very clever. Pattie had been his partner in deception. He felt that that made it excusable to dislike her. He marvelled at the way the affections could change, and felt glad of it. He need not bother about her any more. The cleansing downpour was washing his infatuation away. Even the fear that Burke would arrive at any moment and murder him, even that fear was being washed away.

The rain slackened. He went back into the bedroom and started to look for a towel, without success. Eventually he found a towelling dressing-gown, far too big for him, evidently the property of Burke. He put it on. By now the rain was almost a drizzle. Pattie appeared in the doorway.

'He wants to see you,' she announced.

'Seth?'

'Yes. I've been getting breakfast ready.'

Holding his dressing-gown modestly around him, he followed Pattie out of the room. She led him across the garden, to a small covered area, where Seth was sitting, presiding over a tea-pot, like some strange domestic deity. Then she left them.

'Pattie told me you were still here,' said Seth, pouring the tea. 'I suppose you took advantage of Burke's absence.'

'I did.'

'I saw you standing there in the rain,' remarked Seth. 'A fine sight. However, I have just heard that Burke is coming back earlier than expected; he rang to say that he was leaving Tobago this morning. That means he will be here tonight. Burke doesn't like to be away too long, you see. I told him to take a week, and he got suspicious. Do you know what stupid people do when they get ideas into their heads?'

'Is Burke stupid?' asked Simon.

'He is very stupid. Not stupid like his brother, but stupid in a cunning sort of way. He thinks he is very clever. People defer to him, and I think he thinks they think he is intelligent. It isn't that: they are frightened of him. I told you he was a murderer, didn't I?'

'You did. But you didn't tell me who he killed.'

'In the past he has killed people like himself. But now he's done something I can't understand. He told me on the phone that Payne won't be coming back.'

There was silence. Simon sipped his tea.

'Pattie is frightened,' said Seth. 'She told me so herself. I don't know what Burke has done to Payne –'

'He is his brother. Surely he hasn't –'

'Killed him? Probably not. He's probably decided to let him live on in Tobago, with their aged mother. But you see, Burke

170

must have got something out of that damn fool brother of his. That's what's frightening Pattie.'

'What did she tell Payne? Or what did you tell Payne?'

'Pattie told Payne that he was to steal Burke's gun and give it to you when they got back here. He promised her he would: the fool didn't quite realise what she had in mind. I suppose that was what made him discuss it with Burke. That is what has made him suspicious.'

'I don't understand what you have been up to,' said Simon.

'The plan was that you were going to kill Burke with his own gun,' said Seth.

'That is not going to happen,' said Simon. 'Not now it isn't.'

'We can get other guns,' said Seth.

'No.'

Seth was silent. The blunt refusal made him think. Then, after a magisterial pause, he began to explain.

'I want Burke dead,' he said simply. 'And so do you. He is a dangerous man. He is a criminal. You are not: you can shoot him, and then we'll get rid of the body, and no one will ask any questions. Payne is already out of the way, and we won't have to rely on him. People will assume Payne did it, if they assume anything. Pattie is trustworthy, and we can count on her.'

'You don't understand me,' said Simon, getting up. 'I would rather die than kill anyone, even Burke.'

'Then you may get what you want,' said Seth. 'Because he will kill you when he finds out about you and Pattie. I did warn you that this was dangerous, but you wouldn't listen. And Pattie will tell him. He's a man who has a way of getting information out of people. It has already gone too far.'

Simon sat down again. It had gone too far. Here he was, wearing the man's dressing-gown, having slept with his wife.

'When he comes back here tonight, he will go to bed. He will be tired after his journey. He never wears anything in bed, and the unclothed are always at a disadvantage. He will leave the gun on the bedside table. I can give you a key, you can come in. Pattie can take the gun and you can use it on him. He sleeps on his

171

stomach, and you can shoot him in the back of the head. There won't be much blood as long as you kill him with the first bullet. You ever used a gun before?'

'Never.'

'It is easy enough. You just point it at the back of his head, and pull the trigger. Then we can bury the body in the garden, or we can dump it in the sea. No one will ever know. No one will hear anything either.'

'Have you planned this for a long time?' asked Simon.

'I like to think ahead. When I saw you, I knew that you were the one to replace Burke.'

'And does Pattie want to see him dead?'

'She does. She don't like him that much any more. She prefers you.'

Murder, reflected Simon, was an aphrodisiac of sorts.

'If you do this,' said Seth, 'you will prove yourself. You will show that you are in this with me. It has to be done.'

'I'm in nothing with you,' said Simon.

'But you are. I got rid of Barratt for you. And you didn't complain then. And when I got Da Silva to pay for the Cathedral, you didn't complain either. And this time you must do your own dirty work. Burke will kill you without even asking my permission. I'm losing my grip on him as it is. I've seen the way he looks at you, and I know that he'd love to do it. If, or when, Pattie tells him everything, he won't hesitate. I can't protect you. And if you do kill him, it will be in self-defence,' he concluded, with a flourish worthy of Father Salvatori himself.

'I can't fire a gun,' said Simon.

'Strangle him with a tourniquet or stab him in the jugular; but he's a strong man, and you would be better off learning how to pull a trigger. Even if you miss the first time, he'll be naked and defenceless. But you won't miss; he won't even wake up. It'll be the easiest thing in the world.'

'I've got to go,' said Simon. 'I need to dress.'

'Speak to Pattie first. And take this key. He'll be asleep at midnight.'

172

Seth held out a key. Simon hesitated a moment, and then took it. He made his barefooted way to the bedroom where he had spent the night. Pattie was there, waiting for him. He sat on the bed and began to put on his socks.

'Well?' she asked, putting her arm around his neck. 'Has he explained it to you?'

'He has,' he answered shortly.

'Aren't you going to tell me that you love me?' she asked.

He kept his lips tight-shut and reached for his trousers. Her request was impossible. To love her meant murdering Burke. Her arms grasped him around the waist, impeding his hurried attempts to dress.

'Kill Burke,' said Pattie. 'Please,' she added, raising her lips to be kissed.

'I have to go,' he said prosaically.

And within a moment he was indeed gone, leaving her alone and uncertain.

16

THEY HANGED you for murder in Trinidad, Simon remembered, as soon as he was clear of the house. No enlightened rationalists had persuaded them to abolish the death penalty as they had in England. He wondered what it would be like to be hanged. They said that it was very quick. They came to your cell, tied your hands together behind your back and marched you – generally kicking and screaming – to the scaffold, put the hood over your head, fitted on the noose and pulled the lever. The entire process was supposed to take only thirty seconds. For the sake of efficiency and convenience the condemned cell, where you spent your last three weeks on earth, was next to the execution chamber. They whisked you through the communicating door and sent you post-haste to eternity. The hangman had a special book full of tables of weights and measures, so he could calculate the exact drop needed to kill you. Comforting as all this scientific accuracy was, you still heard disquieting stories about Hangings That Went Wrong. Some prisoners went off their food and lost weight while awaiting execution; others consoled themselves by doing the very opposite, eating everything they could: the results were that either the victim was decapitated, or the executioner had to tug them by the ankles to finish the job. Excessive or insufficient drop both sounded equally fearful.

*

These thoughts accompanied him to the Bishop's house. He wondered if he wasn't getting too het up about the whole thing. He tried to calm himself down. The vast majority of murderers, like Burke, were never caught. People in Port of Spain had bars on their windows because they knew that anyone could come in and chop them up with virtual impunity. Rich white people were murdered all the time, as were poor black ones, and no one ever seemed to pay for it. It was, on balance, unlikely that anyone would even notice the demise of Burke. Pattie and Seth would hardly be likely to inform the police, when they were going to be accessories after the event, or whatever the legal phrase was. They were even going to provide the weapon. And the Chief of Police was in Seth's pocket. He would do nothing, just as he had done nothing the time Burke had shot up Barratt's house. No one would dig up the garden, searching for buried corpses. It would be as if nothing had happened.

It would be exactly the same if he were the victim too. Burke might kill him in the knowledge that no one would punish him for such a crime. As long as Burke was alive, there was that danger, unless he had been greatly deceived and the whole thing was a terrible practical joke. It had that nightmarish unreality about it that made it seem like a joke; but Pattie had seemed serious enough, and that had been real fear that he had seen in her eyes.

He rang the doorbell. It was not opened with its usual promptness. Perhaps there was something wrong. He was about to summon up the courage to ring again, when it was opened by John Salvatori.

'I am glad to see you,' he said. 'Archbishop Alphonsus has just arrived. He's currently in with the Bishop. They're discussing things – you know, important matters. Do come in. Lunch may be a little late, but I am sure you won't mind, will you?'

'No, no, not at all.'

'It will be a pleasant surprise for you, seeing the Archbishop, won't it?'

'Oh yes,' said Simon.

The opposite was true. When one was midway between adultery and murder, the last thing one wanted to have was a meeting with the most virtuous and kind person that you knew.

'What's the matter?' asked Salvatori. 'You are very quiet.'

'The matter is Seth,' said Simon slowly.

'He's not dead or anything, is he?' asked Salvatori, feeling that everything was going wrong at once.

'Oh, he'll never die. The matter is me and you and Seth. It would have been better if I had never gone up there with you.'

'Look, whatever has happened, just let it keep until after lunch, when the Archbishop has left. You don't want to spoil his Christmas, do you?'

'You have already spoilt mine,' said Simon.

'Try and remember that there is honour, even among thieves,' said Salvatori with a touch of desperation. 'We are all in this together.'

'You have landed me in it,' said Simon accusingly.

Father Salvatori felt the need for a drink. But without either the Bishop or the Archbishop present, it might be considered bad form if he were to help himself to one now. The desire for alcohol, fuelled by a rising sense of panic at the thought that Simon would somehow now ruin everything, fought with his deep-seated desire to defer to the hierarchy. Alcohol won.

'Let's have a drink,' he said, turning to the whisky bottle, which had made a festive appearance. 'And try and tell me exactly what you mean by what you've just said.'

'I don't want a drink,' said Simon. 'Seth has decided that I should shoot Burke.'

'Is he mad, or are you?'

'He's serious. He wants to get rid of Burke. He's frightened of him, and he thinks that Burke might ruin him anyway, by doing something foolish. He got Pattie to ask Payne to steal Burke's gun. He said he would, but now it seems that Payne has told Burke all about it; and now Burke is coming back from Tobago wanting revenge, and he's left Payne behind there.'

'But why should that concern you?' asked Salvatori.

'Because Burke will think that I asked Pattie – that's the girl – she's his wife – to steal the gun to kill him with, because I've been making up to her. And if he finds out what I've done with her, he'll kill me. Seth says he's dangerous, and I believe him.'

'So do I,' said Salvatori. He took a gulp of whisky. 'Oh, shit,' he said.

Further conversation was cut short by the entry of Nourganian and the Bishop. Lunch was presently served. In these circumstances, neither John nor Simon was disposed to feel comfortable. Simon felt that this meal might well be the last he would enjoy with a relatively unguilty conscience. And Salvatori, as he chewed his turkey, thought not of the fact that it had been buried underground for five days and that it tasted of earth; rather he thought that Seth had outwitted him, and that somehow or other he had to find a way of escape. The old man had tricked them: he was forcing them to pay a bill Salvatori had thought would never have to be paid. The price to pay was complicity in murder.

The only person truly at ease was Nourganian. Alfred had told him all that had happened, and Nourganian was putting his faith in God.

Lunch was soon over, there having been scant conversation. Alphonsus Nourganian, having praised the turkey, withdrew once more into Alfred's study to talk to him in private, asking the other two to wait for him.

*

'I was thinking about what you told me over lunch,' he said to Alfred once they were safely in the study. 'You called it a vision of darkness. Or else an experience of nothingness. That somehow at the heart of it all there was a big hole, an emptiness. I notice from your desk that you have been reading about Heidegger. That's ruined a lot of people, but perhaps it has saved you. It has given you words, borrowed words, which you can use to describe your – I don't think there's an English word for it. Of course, you couldn't say the words of consecration. You perceived God as absent. I'm not surprised that Salvatori didn't understand you. In an odd sort of way, you have seen something of God.'

'But you said the absence of God, just now,' said Alfred.

177

'No,' said Nourganian firmly. 'I said you perceived God as absent. When you realise someone isn't there, that is another way of saying that they are there no longer, or they are somewhere else. You saw the black hole where God ought to have been. You saw He was not there; but you can't say that a non-existent person isn't there, can you? That would be nonsense. Only a real person can be absent. You still believe in God, don't you?'

'Of course I do.'

'I knew you did. I suppose Salvatori would think that you'd suddenly become an atheist. But in fact you are going in quite the opposite direction. You are discovering God. You are going through the darkness into the light. The darkness you saw, the emptiness, the nothing, was what was inside you. You've been here for twenty years, twenty years of almost Turkish inactivity ...'

The appellation Turkish, coming from an Armenian, was condemnation indeed. And it was true. He had spent twenty years in idleness, doing nothing useful. He might have written all those articles and said Mass in public twice a year, and prayed, but he had done all those things without looking into his own soul, without searching for God. He had been too satisfied with himself, he now realised; a strange realisation, for until now he had always thought of himself as hard on himself: but that had been another form of self-indulgence.

'You see?' said Alphonsus, 'You are being called onwards, forwards. This is what I had hoped.'

'You hoped for it?'

'Yes. When I knew that Simon was coming here, that's what I hoped for; and that is why I sent you John Salvatori. Having Simon here has helped you unlock all those things that you had kept buried away; all those things that you had hoped you would never have to think about again. And as for Salvatori, he made you think about yourself. Odd as it may sound, I think you are rather alike – I mean, when I first saw Salvatori, he reminded me of you as you were twenty-five years ago. Of course, you're quite different when it comes to background, but in essentials, if you see what I mean ...' He paused, and then continued on a new tack. 'Some people would say that you've had a sort of nervous breakdown. They love that phrase nowadays. It is a silly expression. What you have had is a moment of grace, a revelation. God has shown you the truth, what you really are. He is calling you out into the desert ...'

'Haven't I been in the desert already? Isn't San Fernando desolate enough?'

'That's what you always supposed. You saw yourself as exiled. You refused ever to come to Port of Spain; you stayed here for twenty years. You withdrew. That's not a desert. It is a fit of pique. You shut everyone out. You didn't want to see Simon, because it was a painful reminder. And as for Salvatori –'

'You couldn't have chosen a better man,' said Alfred carefully. 'He is what I used to be. Except he has something called, I believe, the common touch; there are a few things you are going to have to sort out there. He's got involved with this hoodlum called Seth, and he seems to have dragged Simon into it too.'

'John is always getting into trouble. He doesn't have your ability to distinguish between people. Even in Port of Spain ... There are two types of priest, you know. There are those who get things done, who build Cathedrals, men with the common touch, as you put it. They are practical men of business – just like those popes who led their troops into battle and sold indulgences to build St Peter's. On the whole, they are the sort of priests that people admire and sometimes even love.'

'And the other type?'

'The other type are by no means so popular. They make people uncomfortable. John is the first type, but you are destined to be the second type. You aren't like him at all, I suppose, despite what I just said. The first type are rarely saints; the second are always martyrs.'

'A martyr? Me?'

'Yes, Alfred, why not? You have seen the dark side of God. You now have to spend the rest of your life making sense of it, working out your salvation with fear and trembling. Other people, people

179

like John, won't have the faintest idea of what you are on about. They just stick to what they know, and they muddle through somehow or other. Think of the Israelites and the Golden Calf. It's had rather a bad press; I like the Golden Calf, and so did they: it was familiar and comforting and rather fun. But what Moses did was terrifying: going up the mountain alone to have a face-to-face interview with the Living God. And once you see something of God, nothing on earth is ever the same again. The mystics are necessary for the Church. But people like John are equally important. There must be someone who will get things done, after all. But it won't be you.'

'I suppose this means I must leave San Fernando,' said Alfred. 'Will that be difficult?'

'Oddly enough, it will. I've never liked it here, you know. But all the same, it is familiar, it is safe and it is what I have known for a long time. Will they make Salvatori the new Bishop?'

'He has the common touch. He's certain to be the new Bishop.'

Alfred smiled. 'And what about me?' he asked.

'You must go into the unknown. I have an idea for you, if you want to do something adventurous.'

'Where?'

'First make up your mind about whether you want to go into the unknown. Then I can tell you about it. Prepare yourself. And if you want to go, prepare to go soon. One can't delay and hum-and-ha when it comes to answering the divine call, you know. You've just got to do it.'

'Even without knowing what it involves?'

'Especially without knowing. You have got to be prepared for any sacrifice. You may find it too much for you. But if you say yes, you won't regret it at all. Renunciation brings great rewards.'

'Do I have to renounce everything? I mean, what about Simon?'

'You will have to renounce him too,' said Nourganian. 'And there's also the question of the boy being provided for with your money.'

180

'I'll do anything you say,' said Alfred.

'Good. And now I'll leave you here and go and have a word with Salvatori.'

*

The Archbishop left the room on silent feet, and Alfred was left alone to his reflections. An enormous sense of peace crept over him. All would be well. The weight of twenty years was falling away from him. He had already renounced all the things that had imprisoned him for so long. The sense of nothingness that he had faced in the Cathedral the night before now seemed a blessing indeed.

Downstairs, the Archbishop was listening to the whole sorry tale, but it was not Salvatori who told it to him. Simon had confessed; there was something about Alphonsus that meant that you could not lie to him, and Simon had told him everything. It was Alphonsus whom he had trusted, after all, for years, long before he had met Salvatori or Seth or Pattie. Alphonsus would now save him from the frightening possibilities that involvement with these three unwelcome new friends had opened up.

'Father Salvatori has not been wise,' said Alphonsus eventually, when he had heard it all. 'Of course, you were not to know it, but his judgment has never been very good. You really must not blame yourself too much. Of course, you have done wrong, but only because you thought that wrong was the right thing to do. But the fact is that you don't belong to Seth at all, and if you had known that from the beginning, then it would have saved you this trouble. Only I suppose that knowledge can never come easily; it always has to be learned the hard way, as they say.'

'But,' said Simon, 'Seth and I are rather similar. Seth says that we're in this together, against people like Mr Barratt. Against the whites, I suppose he meant.'

'People always find race a convenient vehicle for putting people in categories; but it shouldn't be done. There are good men and there are evil ones, and there are many who come be-

181

tween; that is all. And now there is something that I must tell you. You haven't told the Bishop that your mother was called Miss Scott, before she started calling herself Mrs Palmer. That is, I don't suppose you thought it was important. It isn't the sort of thing you mention, is it?'

'Is it important?' asked Simon, wondering why the Archbishop had changed the subject.

'It is. The Bishop once knew your mother. It was a long time ago and he knew her as Miss Maria Scott. He hadn't realised that she was your mother; and I hadn't realised that he had known her. The Bishop can tell you something that will change everything.'

'How?'

'He can tell you who your father was, and thus he can tell you who you are,' said Alphonsus. 'I'll call him down.'

Alphonsus went to summon Alfred.

'You must do as I say exactly,' he told him. 'You must tell him what I tell you to tell him.'

In the short interval he was alone, Simon sat trying to gather his thoughts. He was not sure that he wanted to solve this great mystery after all; but there was something about Nourganian, now coming into the room with Bishop Palmer-Ross obediently behind, which made him realise that whatever Nourganian might do would be for the best.

'Now,' said Alphonsus, 'tell Simon about Maria Scott.'

Alfred looked at the young man for a moment, and began to speak:

'My parents had a house in Tobago. Their main house was in Maraval. It has been knocked down now and built over, so you wouldn't know where to look for it now. The same has happened to the house in Tobago. That was where Maria Scott was the housekeeper; it was a cocoa estate which never made any profit, and she looked after the house, which we hardly ever used. We used to go there about once a year, I seem to remember. When my father died the place was sold. That was when Miss Scott stopped working for my family.'

182

'How many brothers and sisters did you have?' asked Alphonsus. 'Tell him about them; tell him what happened to them all.'

'I have a sister who married an Englishman and lives with him in England. She's the eldest and she must be about sixty now. Then there's John who went to Australia, and then there's me. Then there's Anthony who lives in Canada – he used to be in insurance in Port of Spain. And then there was Hugo, who was rather wild and killed himself in a car crash when he was about your age. He never married. He's been dead nearly thirty years, but all the others are married with children, but none of them here in Trinidad apart from myself.'

'And who bought the fent-shop for Maria?' asked Alphonsus. 'Answer.'

'I did.'

'There,' said Alphonsus. 'Now let me tell him why. The Bishop – though he was only Father Palmer-Ross then – bought the shop for your mother. That is to say, he was the one who paid for it.'

'Why?' asked Simon.

'At the time your mother was pregnant with you, and he felt that he was responsible for her. You see, Hugo had been killed in a car crash and the Bishop was tidying up his affairs. It was Hugo who was your father. So Alfred bought the shop for your mother. At least he put up the money. After that she changed her name, and he never heard from her again.'

'I never heard from her again,' echoed Alfred.

'You are my uncle,' said Simon.

Alphonsus looked at Alfred.

This then was the sacrifice that was to be asked of him.

Simon was looking at him expectantly, his face alive with curiosity, and never more than at that moment did it seem to Alfred that to have had a son would have been an enormous comfort; and that to live in the knowledge that he had a son who was destined never to know him a most terrible loss. He was fifty-six years old, and he felt the years weigh down upon him all of a sudden. In the years that remained, who would be there to comfort him?

He hesitated, and he felt Nourganian's eyes upon him. He knew that the renunciation had to be made. Fifty-six was too old to become a father for the first time. The moment of hesitation was passing. He would lie. The Archbishop knew best, and he had promised to trust Nourganian.

'You are my uncle?' Simon was saying, repeating himself, as if to try and get used to this strange new relationship.

'Yes,' lied the Bishop.

'And why did my mother never tell me?'

'She kept a prudent silence,' said Alphonsus. 'Hugo was dead. He couldn't marry her, you see. She didn't want to apply to the family for more money, though she could have done. In fact she deliberately chose to cut herself off from them.'

'But why?' asked Simon.

'I think she must have thought the whole thing was too painful to mention,' said Alphonsus. 'I think she loved Hugo. She carried around the tragedy of his death, the fact that he could never be with her again, until she died herself. He was a very handsome and charming man. He was quite famous for it in Trinidad.'

'Poor mother,' said Simon. 'Then she did love him?'

'Yes,' said Alfred. 'I am sure she must have done.'

'And did he love her?'

Alphonsus looked towards Alfred.

'Yes, he did,' said Alfred. 'Hugo was a very generous man; of course, he didn't leave a will or anything like that, but he didn't expect to die. But he was my brother, and he was the closest to me in age. I knew after he was dead that he would have wanted me to help her. I wished I could have done more.'

'Good,' said Alphonsus. 'There is something about love that I have noticed, and that is that it is bounded by silence. She never told you about it, because she didn't have the words to express what it meant. It was beyond words; and the highest sort of love always entails keeping silence, a prudent silence.'

Alfred looked away.

'I should be glad to have an uncle and all those relations everywhere,' said Simon at last.

'I am glad that there is now one other Palmer-Ross in Trinidad,' said Alfred. 'I've got all sorts of things that I don't need myself –'

'I was coming to that,' said Alphonsus. 'You see now, Simon, why there is no reason for you to stay here any longer. Seth and all these other people are now in the past and you have left them all behind.'

'Yes,' said Simon. 'It is strange.'

'You could go to university in England,' said Alfred. 'You could become a doctor or a lawyer or whatever, and I could pay for it all, very happily …'

'All that can be discussed later,' said Alphonsus. 'You can come with me to Port of Spain tonight, but before all that I'd better go and ask Father Salvatori whether he wants to be the next Bishop of San Fernando. I wonder what his answer will be?'

Alphonsus left the room.

'Are you going too?' asked Simon.

'Yes.'

'Where to?'

'Somewhere new. I don't quite know where yet, but I am looking forward to it already.'

'That sounds just like me,' said Simon. 'If you are going to leave Trinidad, perhaps we could go together?'

'Yes, that would be – pleasant, I was going to say. But I don't think we had better do it. You have to go and discover what your new life will be, and so have I, and we will have to do that separately, I think.'

'Why?' asked Simon.

'I don't quite know,' said Alfred. 'It is hard to explain. Perhaps I wouldn't be good for you. I do have near relations, but they are all far away. I would end up by making too much of you. I would smother your growth. You've got a future ahead of you. You're bright, and you're sensible and you're intelligent and you are good-looking. You are full of promise, just as Hugo was. What you are going to be all lies in the future, and I am something from your past.'

185

'But you are my uncle.'

'Yes, I have to get used to thinking of you as my nephew. But you must be yourself and not just someone else's nephew, or even someone else's son. That is what your mother wanted. She wanted you to be yourself and to be free, not trapped by the past. Of course, you must know about the past, but you mustn't carry it around with you too much.'

'What should I do then?'

'Go and do all the things that I might have done if I were you,' urged Alfred. 'Go to England for a start, and from there discover the world.'

'Do they like black people in England?' asked Simon a little doubtfully.

'Don't let that worry you. Don't be limited by those thoughts. You will be yourself and that will be enough and more than enough. Don't think in the way people like Seth think. You're not an outsider.'

'You are right. I've always thought little of myself up to now. It never really occurred to me that the thought of my father being an English gentleman could possibly be true.'

'He wasn't English and he wasn't a gentleman. He was as Trinidadian as you are, and he was liked by everyone.'

'Good,' said Simon. 'I like the sound of him already. And now even the thought of Seth seems a little unreal.'

17

'What will happen to him?' asked Alfred, as evening drew on.

'Isn't he here?' asked Alphonsus, to whom this question was addressed, and who had only just come into the room.

'He has gone home to pack,' said Alfred. 'Packing is a rather doleful activity, I always find. It has such finality.'

'But not for him, perhaps,' said Alphonsus. 'I really don't know what will happen to him. He will have his own life. He's intelligent and he's been reasonably well educated up to now, and so we must hope that he'll make the best of it. He's free to choose, something he wasn't before. He never quite knew how he was meant to fit in, but now he does, and so he has somewhere to start out from.'

'But you lied to him,' said Alfred. 'He isn't Hugo's, is he?'

'Of course he isn't, and I didn't mean to rewrite history. It was a lie, I suppose, but I'd rather say that what I did tell him was true in substance. His father was a rich, white man called Palmer-Ross, who through no fault of his own couldn't marry his mother. All that is true. To have told him that his father was a Bishop would have done untold harm, I think. He has to be free. His father is to all intents and purposes dead to him. We have to let him go.'

'We?'

'You and I. Oh, you'll hear from him from time to time and perhaps you will see him occasionally. But he will grow up away from you. He has to; he will be himself, not your son, or your anything. And he won't be mine either; he won't be my protégé, the Archbishop's little charity case, any more. Nor will Seth have possession of him, or even Salvatori. Perhaps I will never see him

187

again, but we have to let people we love be free. We can't imprison them or make them be what we want them to be. I had rather hoped that he would be a priest, you know, but that was my ambition and not his. We have to let go.'

Alfred listened to Nourganian and felt a ray of illumination entering his mind, as through an opening door. He had known Nourganian for years, ever since the old man had become Archbishop, but only now did he see that he had never really known the man as he was. Nourganian would miss Simon. He had, in the old phrase, been like a father to him. Alfred knew that he was witnessing a renunciation more profound than his own. The things that he was to give up were nothing to this. He felt the stirrings of compassion. He was only losing what might have been, and what he knew could never be; but Nourganian was renouncing, not twenty wasted years, but twenty years of affection and mutual understanding.

'I am sorry,' said Alfred, not knowing what to say, yet feeling that silence was more inadequate than even these inadequate words.

'Yes, it is a sacrifice,' said Nourganian eventually. 'But I will take him to Port of Spain tonight, and no doubt he will be quite eager to get on the next plane out of Piarco. I suppose we had better talk about Salvatori ...'

Nourganian spoke about Salvatori: how, though in many respects rather a weak man, he would nevertheless make a good Bishop. How Salvatori was a man of his time, and for his time. How the Church needed men like Salvatori as Bishops. How the people loved him. How Salvatori had the 'common touch'.

'And as for you yourself,' concluded the Archbishop, 'I seem to remember that you speak excellent French.'

'Yes, I do,' admitted Alfred.

'Those articles of yours were really quite good. I read them all, you know,' said Nourganian. 'Now, didn't someone tell me that you were once learning Arabic?'

'I never got very far with it though,' said Alfred. 'That was when I was in Rome; I did it in tandem with Hebrew.'

'Now Arabic,' said Nourganian, 'is rather an easy language to pick up. I learned it off my grandmother, you know, when I was a little boy. It is rather a useful language, don't you think?'

Alfred wondered where this was leading. Little by little, Nourganian outlined his plans for him. He listened attentively and felt that San Fernando and Trinidad itself were receding into the distance already.

*

Darkness came, and with it a sense of uneasiness for Mr Seth. He sat by his swimming-pool, staring into the black waters, anxious and doubtful. Burke had once been a good boy to him, fifteen years ago. When he had discovered him, Burke had been a promising young thug. Seth had more or less adopted him, just as he himself had once been adopted by another man.

That other man had been Tony Singh.

I am getting old, thought Seth. He had always suspected that when old age came, Tony Singh would come back to haunt him. And he was thinking of Tony Singh a great deal now. It was morbid, the way his mind dwelled on Singh, but he couldn't help it. Tony had been good to him. When Tony had discovered him, Seth had just been a small-timer. There had been a few profitable ventures – extortion, theft from the Port of Spain docks, the odd hit – but in those days Seth had been a lone shark. It had been Tony who had convinced him that unity was strength, and that he was better off with Tony to protect him, and after that he had become Tony's man. Rewards had followed, such rewards, and with them the inevitable resentment that accompanies the unequal division of spoils. Naturally Tony had been the boss, but it had been Seth who had done the work and run the risks. He had been the one who had had to deal with the uncooperative, but it had been Tony who had benefited and made all the money. Seth had raised this point, and the parting of the ways had resulted. He became a lone shark again, hunting on his own, but the

189

resentment continued. Failing to be friends, they had become rivals; rivals had a way of turning into enemies.

That was why Seth had had to kill him.

He had never dreamed that killing the old man would have been so difficult. He had never imagined that such a struggle would be possible. He had hoped that the old man would have died quietly, overcome by a single stab wound. But Singh was a fighter to the last; despite the stab wound in his stomach he had retaliated with the only weapon that had come to hand: namely, a metal Parker pen that he kept on his desk. (For the old man had let Seth into his house for the final interview, thinking that he was seeking a reconciliation, so much had pride undone him.)

The metal pen had cost Seth his eye; inexpert surgery on an infected wound had resulted in the disfigurement around the empty socket. It had made him fearful and feared. His scars, like those of a gladiator, had established him as a man of repute. From then on he had never looked back, but had become one of the most feared men in Trinidad, stepping right into Tony Singh's still warm shoes.

Now, this Christmas night, the feared man was himself afraid. For just as he had turned against his erstwhile protector, he now knew that Burke was turning against him.

Seth, despite being a benefactor of the Church, was not a man who could be described as religious. He had little idea of Divine Justice, but he did believe in Fate. Burke would try and kill him, just as he had killed Tony Singh. Nor was this all; it was not just that it was the rule that subordinates rose up against their masters, just as sons rebelled against their fathers: recently he had seen Burke looking at him, sizing him up, calculating the risks, looking for his opportunity.

Seth knew, as he gazed into his black swimming-pool, that time was running out on him. Gone were the happy days when a Tony Singh could rule Port of Spain and make fools of the police. Organised crime was now a failing business. In Port of Spain things had been quiet for a long time. Only in San Fernando – thanks to the Chief of Police, thanks to the fact that no one

190

outside the place cared a damn about what went on there – only in San Fernando was a little honest business still possible. Every business in the place paid him something. But the business of frightening people into parting with their cash on a regular basis, Burke's métier, was fast going out of date. The future lay in contraband; the future belonged to clever men who could handle paperwork, men who could arrange for forbidden goods that they would never see to be shipped from one place to another. Burke was all very well, but a brainless thug would hardly be a match for the Americans who made it their business to interrupt the trade routes between Colombia and Miami. Brainless thugs were indiscreet and tended to attract unwelcome attention. How different was Simon Palmer. He was clever. Mr Seth sighed at the prospect of making his business into something almost legal in its slickness. Someone like Simon would be able to handle cocaine as easily as Da Silva handled cement.

*

Pattie, meanwhile, was in her part of the house, watching television. The local stations, though she knew no others, generally left her unsatisfied. She had flicked through the various channels, rejecting a film, *Bridge Over the River Kwai*, which she seemed to remember having seen before, and an adaptation of a Barbara Cartland novel, which didn't suit her present mood. She alighted on a musical programme. A white lady in a stetson was singing 'Stand By Your Man'. This did suit her mood, and as Pattie listened to the words of the song, two large tears trickled down her cheeks. She couldn't help herself. Pattie had no real theological insights – she wasn't that sort of girl – but nevertheless she knew something about 'the meaning of Christmas'. Christmas, she had learned over the years, meant the Family. It meant the Family with a capital 'F', an idealised Family, the type that did not quite exist, at least not in her world.

Her own family life had been far from ideal: she had been only too glad to throw in her lot with Burke when she had reached the age of eighteen. She was now twenty-three, and five years had not dimmed her memories of home life. When she thought of the past, she realised that Burke had been good to her. He hadn't hit her much or refused to give her money, or neglected her. Burke was a rough diamond, not really a man for much chat, but all the same, whatever his faults, a certain loyalty remained. You were meant to stand by your man, even when you didn't like him any more, simply because he was your man. The trouble was, she hadn't. Her mind went back to the fact that she had asked Payne to steal Burke's gun; she remembered the last night too; that memory made her shiver with guilt. Burke would be furious when he found out what she had done for the Boss. She had been a fool to trust Payne and a fool to trust Simon. And unless Simon and Payne or one or the other killed Burke, Burke would surely kill her.

She thought of Simon. She had done what the Boss had told her to do. She had let Simon do what he wanted to do with her. The picture of it was still in her mind, burning in her conscious-ness. She remembered how he had rolled away from her, turned his back and gone to sleep. She had sensed the contempt he had surely felt for her. (In fact he had felt contempt, but it had not been for her, but for himself, but she was not to know this.) Pattie wondered if she had been right to throw in her lot with Simon and the Boss and with Payne. What would happen to her? At least with Burke she knew where she stood. And what had Payne told Burke? Had he told him about the gun? For Burke was coming back, alone, without Payne.

She looked at the clock. It was nine. Burke would be back in a couple of hours at the latest.

From the garden she heard the Boss calling her. She went out to him.

'Pattie-girl,' he said.

'Yes, Mr Seth?'

The television continued its noise in the background.

'You won't forget what you've got to do?' asked the old man.

'No, sir.'

'When he puts his gun under the pillow when he goes to bed,

you get it and put it where he won't be able to get at it in a hurry. As for the body, we'll have to drive down to the sea and give it to the sharks – if they'll eat it.'

The sharks, remembered Seth, had turned their noses up at Tony Singh.

Pattie looked at Seth and realised he was an old man, worrying over details.

'You want some whisky, boss?' she asked solicitously. 'Let me bring you some whisky: it will help you pass the time until you want to sleep.'

'Yes, Pattie-girl, you get the whisky,' said Seth, moved by this daughterly concern.

She went into the house and came back with the bottle.

'What if Simon doesn't come?' she asked, for somehow, remembering how he had left her that morning, she doubted that he would come. Seth's worries were infectious.

'He'll come,' said Seth.

Silently Pattie filled a glass full of whisky for the old man, and settled down to wait with him. The dark swimming-pool was as calm and as tranquil as a mirror.

*

Less than a mile away, Alfred Palmer-Ross sat on his verandah with his successor.

'I still think it unusual that it should be hot at Christmas,' he said. 'I suppose it must be the influence of all those carols.'

'Yes,' said John Salvatori.

'But I am no longer sorry about it,' continued Alfred. 'I used to be – once. You see, England is only one way of looking at Christmas, and Trinidad another. The real Christmas is in Palestine if it is anywhere at all on earth. That is the mystery, and all the Christmas carols are purely what we make of it. Do you think you will make a good Bishop, John?'

'I think so,' said Salvatori, overcoming his surprise at being asked so direct a question. 'They say I am good with people. That is what Alphonsus said to me this afternoon.'

Alfred thought this over. He himself had never been 'good with people'. He realised that without difficulty. But John Salvatori was a different matter. He had already won so many people over: Mr Seth, Simon and, oddly enough, Alfred himself. This doubtless made him into an ideal modern Bishop. The qualifications for the job had changed; one could not imagine St Augustine or Pius XII being good with people. But those days were gone.

'The Church has changed,' said Alfred. 'I don't think they realised just how much it would change, but it has; it has changed without our quite knowing why, without our being able to do much about it.'

'You have to move with the times,' said John, enunciating this cliché as if it were a great truth. 'The times can't be held back.'

'I'm not in love with the modern age,' said Alfred. 'It is brutal.'

'What do you mean?'

'I mean people like our Mr Seth. And all these people who seem only to be out for their own advantage.'

'There's nothing so very modern about that,' said John. 'These things have always existed. In the Middle Ages there were those robber barons ...'

'Of course there were. I'm not lamenting the good old days that never existed. The present is brutal and all times have been brutal after their own fashion. And they say, and I believe it, that all people believe their own time to be the worst of times. Some try and make the best of it. You are one of those, John. Others try and opt out all together, and shut out the wickedness of the world. I suppose I was one of those. But really, this time we are in isn't a time at all. We are between times, in a sort of long interval, as at the cinema. The first act has happened and we are waiting for the last act to begin; we're in a sort of suspended animation. The first time was in Galilee, when the words 'The Time has come' were said: not just a time but *the* time. And the second time is the second coming.'

194

'And how is this time we are in different?' asked John. 'And if it is, is it important?'

'It is very important,' said Alfred. 'We may live in time, but the Church is eternal, outside time. We have to make the time real, and see that beyond all this lie the eternal truths.'

'Like?'

'The Incarnation — it wasn't hundreds of years ago, it is now, forever and always.'

'I think I see what you mean,' said John. 'But someone has still got to run the Church, haven't they? And the Church has to live in the world. That is where I come in.'

'Yes,' said Alfred. 'There are two jobs to be done. I am sure you will do very well here. I wish you luck. It is almost eleven. I suppose I ought to go to bed as tomorrow I will be off.'

'Where to?'

'I will write and tell you when I get there. I'm not so sure where I am going at present.'

He went into the house, and as he crossed the hallway, he heard a car speed past outside. This was unusual. The car contained Burke.

*

Burke had had a wasted journey. He had been to Tobago to see his aged mother, just as Seth had suggested he might do. The circumstances of the journey, Seth's insistence that he take his brother, had awakened suspicions in that little used organ, Burke's mind. On the boat across to Tobago, Payne had been induced to tell him what was afoot, and how Pattie had asked him to steal his gun. Generously, Burke had decided not to kill Payne, but had left him in Tobago with the solemn warning that if he ever set foot on Trinidad again he would pay for it. Then he had driven back to San Fernando, feeling distinctly less generous to his Boss and his wife.

He felt wounded at the ingratitude of it all as he opened the metal gates, drove in the car and carefully shut the gates behind him. He stopped and listened, like a nocturnal animal. All he

195

could hear was the faint sound of the water lapping in the swimming-pool. He put a reassuring hand on his gun and then crept round the side of the house. A light was on. The girl Pattie was sitting alone by the side of the pool, in the covered chair that usually was only used by Seth. At her feet lay an empty bottle of whisky. She had not noticed the approach of her husband.

'Why are you still up?' he asked.

Her face turned towards him, but she said nothing. He knew now that something was wrong; that she sensed he had come back looking for revenge.

'I have a good mind to kill you,' said Burke in a level voice.

'I know,' she whispered.

'Where is the Boss? Asleep?'

'No,' said Pattie.

And then Burke noticed the body in the water. His grip on his gun relaxed.

'Good girl,' he said. 'We got the place to ourselves at last.'

18

MR SETH'S FUNERAL was the first real event of civic importance to take place in the new Cathedral, and the first to be presided over by the new Bishop-elect, who had had the place built. Monsignor Salvatori thought that this was most appropriate.

The ceremony took place in the second week in January. The body had been embalmed to ensure its preservation. The delay in burying it had been caused by the wait for the Cathedral's windows, for no one had quite wanted to hold a funeral in a windowless concrete shed. In addition, Burke, who was making the arrangements, had rather hoped that the time lapse would ensure a quiet funeral, for there had been considerable interest when it had become known that Mr Seth had died. Such a death, of its very nature, had to be followed by an interregnum of sorts, while Burke had established his new position of power. In the event, all had gone smoothly. Seth had left no will, but no one wanted to dispute Burke's ownership of the estate, and all those who had done business with Seth now seemed equally keen to do business with Burke.

Various theories abounded about what exactly had happened to the late Mr Seth. The disappearance of Payne led most people to assume that he had murdered the old man. Hardly anyone at all believed the official version, namely that the old man had fallen into his swimming-pool and drowned after having drunk too much whisky.

Monsignor Salvatori had his own ideas about the death of his late patron. Mr Seth, as he lay in his white coffin, surrounded by a frilly satin shroud, resembled an ancient Egyptian Pharaoh. He was small, black and leathery, a harmless little mannikin. He had shrunk. How frail human things were, reflected Monsignor Salvatori, as he blessed the cadaver. The odour of incense mingled with the odour of formaldehyde. But the new Cathedral, that was a concrete achievement, and it had not cost a cent. It would still be there long after the memory of Seth had perished. These were the Monsignor's comforting reflections.

The funeral was very well attended. The congregation listened to the readings in hushed reverence. They were treated to the story of Jael and Sisera, and to Our Lord's own words about how those who lived by the sword died by it. Mr Barratt greatly enjoyed hearing how the enterprising Jael had driven a tent peg into Sisera's head; he was sitting half way down the nave, and was enjoying himself. Perhaps he would start coming to church again, now that he had taken up his old job with Da Silva once more. He had already spoken to Burke and found that the man was quite keen to deal with the small matter of Mr Seth's debt.

The truth was that Burke was something of a traditionalist. He was never happier than when he was doing what he was best at, extortion. But he had no desire to expand into what his late master had thought of doing, namely racketeering. Burke was a simple soul: brutal and violent, but not very clever. Pattie realised this. Now that she had committed a murder all of her own, she noticed that he was beginning to look at her in a new way. He was beginning to respect her, and treat her as an equal. She did not quite know why, but this left her a little depressed. She knew Burke feared his equals. An equal might turn into a rival at a moment's notice and try to stab you in the back. Burke was now on his guard against her; when he slept he did so alone now, in a locked room, with his gun always on his bedside table. He had done so ever since that Christmas night, when she had pushed the old man into the water and held his head under until he had stopped struggling. How he had struggled. If she had known what the result was going to be, perhaps she would have helped him out of the water, as he had pleaded with her to do, until she had silenced him. The old curse, which she had first heard as a child, had come back to her. Her longing was for her husband, but he was lording it over her. He was looking at her with suspicious eyes and would never trust her again. Simon Palmer had not trusted her either, in the end. Only one person had trusted her – and she had drowned him. Pattie shed a silent tear for Mr Seth, while the Bishop-elect sprinkled the coffin with holy water, which was supposed to symbolise the waters of baptism, the waters of rebirth. But Pattie wept, remembering the dark swimming-pool and the chance of love that she had thrown away for ever.

19

SIMON PALMER was writing to the man he had begun to think of as 'Uncle Alfred'. He sat at his desk which commanded a fine view of the meadows and which was illuminated by gentle English sunshine. It was what the English called summer, the month he had heard described as 'flaming' June. He was dressed in thick grey flannels, a white cotton shirt, a tweed jacket and heavy black shoes. This was his second summer in England, but he still felt the cold. His desk was covered with books, most of them novels, a few of poetry, books with which he had now become familiar.

'The exams are over for this year,' he had written, 'and they went much as I expected. The Shakespeare paper was good fun, if you can believe that. I was thinking of going to Trinidad this summer, but I have been persuaded by someone to go to France instead, for a month, and then from there, perhaps, on somewhere else. We shall have to see. The someone in question is a girl I have met called Celestria. Her parents have a house in France. They have one in London too; I was there a few weeks ago and met someone whom you may have known: a lady called Pat something or other, who told me that she was a Barratt from Trinidad. We talked about Trinidad in a general way ...'

He could hardly remember Trinidad any more; apart from the abiding cold, there was nothing about England that seemed new or strange. He felt he had been there forever. To think about Trinidad was an exercise in archaeology: it was as dim and distant as some forgotten land, buried by time.

After a little thought, Simon picked up his pen and began to write afresh: 'The only news that I have heard from Trinidad is that Bishop Salvatori is the hot favourite to succeed Archbishop

Alphonsus; I am sure that that won't surprise you. The Arch-bishop himself is going to be in England soon on holiday, celebrating his retirement, and I will see him then. That is one reason why I don't think that I really need to go to Trinidad this summer. It is a pity that you yourself aren't coming here at all soon; Celestria was saying that it was very mysterious that I had no living relations. I told her that I had an uncle who was a Bishop, and she said that she had to meet him; it seems she is very keen on Bishops, and she looked you up in the *Annuario Pontificio*. When she saw where you lived, she suggested we come out to visit you; perhaps next year. Celestria is very keen to see your part of the world ...'

20

'Celestria,' read Alfred a week later, 'is very keen to see your part of the world. She had an uncle out there years ago in some Colonial police force, or was it the war, I forget which. Celestria is very good with reference books, as you must have gathered by her research in the *Annuario Pontificio*; she looked up Palmer-Ross in an old copy of *The Landed Gentry* and found someone who I think must be my great-grandfather in the knightage, giving the address simply as 'Maraval, Trinidad'. I think you will like her a great deal when you meet her ...'

Alfred put the letter to one side. He had read it several times now. It was pleasant to think of these young lives unfolding so many miles away. He had not thought that his money would ever be put to such good use. Not for the first time he reflected on how much Simon talked about this Celestria girl, who had quite replaced Jane Austen and Shakespeare in his affections. He marvelled at the ardour of youth.

He turned back to his work in hand. He was finishing off a lecture which he would deliver the next day. He was writing it in French, the language it would be delivered in. Gently he blew away the white dust that had settled on the paper in the last few moments. There was a lot of dust about in this city: it came from all the repair work that was going on. The dust was accompanied by noise, but he had grown used to that. As he straightened the piles of paper on his desk, he was hardly aware of the bulldozers and cement-mixers throbbing away in the vicinity, outside the library windows. At least now there were windows. When he had first arrived there had been no windows in the building at all: in his bedroom there had been only a hole, a large circular rough-edged shell-hole. He had been a little disconcerted by it; only later had he realised that he had been given the best room in the house, and that some of the others were actually sleeping in rooms that had lost entire walls. Even now, in these days of peace, the odd bomb that people had forgotten about went off in the quietness of the night, just to remind one of the novelty of peace. They called these arbitrary explosions 'making bombs safe'; most people slept through them. They had heard worse in the preceding years, and now they were rejoicing in new-found peace.

The library he sat in was a fine room, happily largely intact: he had chosen to work down there as it was convenient for consulting the many-volumed *Summa Theologica* of St Thomas Aquinas. The ceiling above his head had been painted to show the glory of Heaven, which, in the artist's vision of things, consisted of an orchestra of angels surrounding the Lamb upon his throne; it was decorated with sacred texts in Greek, Latin, Coptic and Armenian. He glanced up at it as he had grown into the habit of doing, as if for inspiration; then he settled down to write the last few paragraphs of the lecture. It was supposed to deal with Aquinas's doctrine of the soul: the soul sought loving union with God, divesting itself of all earthly loves, once it had discovered this one great love that surpasses all others. This, Alfred thought, was an easy concept, but one which was nevertheless something hard to learn. How would he convey that in French? He thought in English; he began to write in French; and tomorrow his students would understand it if they did at all, in their own language, Arabic, for the most part.

Alfred wrote about the nature of divine love for a few moments, distilling his knowledge into the elegant precision of French; then he put down his pen, hoping that something of what he himself had learned would be passed on to the students of the Catholic Seminary of Beirut.

And above his head the angels blew on their silent trumpets in a symphony of praise.

on a phra— by bd at praol t
Jubs fink ?
Jue ten arals fink v
Jave sten prad faals last x

→ royal engrales —
Bozer up tom — Radly

Sea Pern — 31,000 inhallids